BAD WEATHER, BAD MAN

The Curious Librarian Cozy Mystery #2

A Novel By
Zana Hart

East Baton Rouge Parish Library
Baton Rouge, Louisiana

COPYRIGHT

COPYRIGHT © 2014 Hartworks, Inc.

All rights reserved. This book or any portion thereof may not be reproduced or used in any manner whatsoever without the express written permission of the publisher except for the use of brief quotations in a book review.

This is a work of fiction. There are a few similarities to real life, based largely on the author's career as a librarian, but they are disguised.

Silvermine is a fictitious small town in Colorado, bearing similarities to Salida and Alamosa.

Cover photos of librarian and bad man by Kelly Hart. The librarian is an actual library director. Cover design by Zana and Kelly Hart.

Hartworks, Inc., PO Box 632, Crestone, CO 81131

TABLE OF CONTENTS

1: DEATH	1
2: BARB	7
3: POTLUCK	10
4: PARTY	14
5: MURDER	19
6: SUNDAY	23
7: CONVERSATIONS	28
8: REFLECTIONS	32
9: ACE	35
10: OKAY	40
11: FURIOUS	43
12: ANOTHER	48
13: CAMP	52
14: HIKE	56
15: TALKING	60
16: MOMO	63
17: BOARD	69
18: BROTHERS	73
19: THIRTY	77
20: QUESTION	80
21: UPHILL	84
22: ALONE	88
23: HELP	91
24: SEARCH	95
25: HOSPITAL	99
26: BROKEN	104
27: FLOOD	108

28: THRILLERS	112
29: HOME	115
30: BETTER	118
31: EMAIL	122
32: ALIBI	126
33: READING	131
34: OMG	135
35: FORWARD	139
36: RETURN	142
37: AWAY	147
38: WOMEN	151
39: BUSINESS	155
40: MOTEL	160
41: SURPRISE	164
42: BYE	168
43: DREAMS	175
FROM THE AUTHOR	179

1: DEATH

A MAN STOOD just inside the front door of the Silvermine Public Library, staring at the row of computers as if they were from another world. Thin, with a wrinkled face, and of medium height, he was wearing layers of shirts, old jeans, a hoodie, and a full daypack. Lauren Long, the library director, was glad that Grace Johnson happened to be working at the front desk, as both Grace and the man were African-American. Most of the minorities in the Colorado town were Hispanics, and Lauren guessed that Grace's presence would make the man less likely to bolt. But Grace was helping someone else, and the man looked nervous. Lauren figured he was likely from the homeless camp just outside of town, in the forest.

She left the reference desk and asked the man if she could help him.

"I have to send an email," he said. "But I don't know about computers and I don't type too good."

"Come sit down at this one, and I'll type for you, if you don't mind my knowing what you say," she said.

"No ma'am, that's fine. Here's a paper Billy gave me to keep."

"Oh yes, I know Billy. He uses the library," Lauren said.

The man looked directly at her for the first time and said, "Pleased to meet you. My name is Lee."

"Hi, Lee, I'm Lauren."

The wrinkled scrap of paper had Billy's email address at gmail plus his password and then another email address. Lauren guided Lee to a lounge chair at the end of the row of computers, and she opened a browser window on the nearest computer. She opened Billy's account, put the other email in, and looked at Lee.

He dictated slowly, struggling for his words. "Dear Barb, Billy was killed last night at the bridge. I'll tell you what happened when you get here. Can you come right away?" Lee started to cry, wiped his tears on the sleeve of his jacket, and cried more noisily. A young woman using a nearby computer glanced over at him and quickly turned away.

"Oh, I'm so sorry," Lauren said. "I was just talking with Billy yesterday."

Lee asked, "What was he talking about?"

"He was doing an email to his cousin and he told me his friends got him a nice cake for his birthday."

"I got the cake," Lee said. "Billy was my friend and he just turned fifty."

"I'm about to have a birthday, too," Lauren said, trying to make Lee feel more at home. "But I'll just be thirty." That felt pretty old to her.

Lee said, "Thirty? I wouldn't have thought you were that old. You've got your whole life ahead of you, if you don't mind my saying so, ma'am. What else did Billy talk about?"

"Umm…" Lauren made a split-second decision to tell Lee. "He warned me about someone he called a bad man. He said the guy shouldn't be allowed in the library."

"That could be one of the guys out at the camp. Did he tell you a name?"

"No, it started to rain and he left. But back to this email, it's to his cousin, right? Do you want her to answer before she comes, or is there anything else you want to tell her now?"

Lee looked confused. "I don't think so," he said. "She'll know what to do. She always does."

Lauren said, "Let's give her my email too, and also the phone here at the library, just in case."

"Thank you," he said, tears still glistening on his wrinkled cheeks.

The next morning, Lauren went to work early to get some uninterrupted time to work on the budget before the library opened. She made a cup of coffee and settled in the small staff workroom downstairs. Just over a hundred years old, the Carnegie library was crowded but homey. With the heavy rains this fall, there were several places where the roof leaked, and there were windows that let water in when the wind blew against them. Lauren looked out the window at the golden patches of aspen trees in the nearby mountains. She enjoyed their beauty for a moment before tackling her work.

When the phone rang, she was annoyed at losing her concentration but answered it automatically. A gravel-voiced woman said, "This is Billy's cousin Barb. Thanks for helping Lee out. Tell him I'll come today and I'll go find him near the bridge tomorrow morning. How was he when you saw him?"

"In tears," Lauren said.

"He's such a dear, I'm not surprised. What have they done with Billy's body? Did Lee tell you anything? I don't want them to toss it in a trash bag and send it to the dump like a dead dog."

Lauren was taken aback by the analogy, but she could easily relate to the emotion in Barb's voice. She found it impossible to accept that most people didn't seem to like the homeless using the library.

"I expect the dead homeless get better treatment than dead dogs," she said. "Lee didn't say anything about the body. He seemed in shock."

"No wonder. I am too. Lee is like family to us, though I'm Billy's only close kin. Billy and I grew up together. Lee's been here to our ranch—I'm in Wyoming—quite a few times with Billy. I wanted them both to live here but Billy was always independent. If you can give me a phone number of a funeral home, I'll call them and the sheriff, and I'll get Billy cremated. Guess I'll see what anyone will tell me about how Billy was killed, while I'm at it. But when you're gone, you're gone and I don't think the world is going to care much about how Billy left it."

Barb outlined her plans. "I'll be coming to Silvermine to throw a big party for Billy. Not a funeral, no way, a real party with food and music and booze and pot and dancing till late. Do you know where there's a good hall to rent in Silvermine, one where they aren't uptight when we crank the music up loud? I'll bring CDs of Billy's favorite music. We're the same age so I've got a lot of them, Michael Jackson, Madonna, The Police, Prince, Marvin Gaye... oh, I'll start out with Springsteen's *Born in the USA*. He nails Billy's story all right."

Lauren couldn't get a word in edgewise. That didn't matter, as Barb had more to say.

"I don't care what the hall costs. Guess we'll do it Saturday night. You're invited, of course. You got a boyfriend or husband or something? Bring 'em along too."

Lauren said, "Thanks, I'll see if my boyfriend wants to go with me. I'm sorry, I don't know about the halls, but our janitor is here and he might know. Just a minute... I'll ask him to pick up another phone."

Richard seemed to have heard the whole conversation. Maybe he had already been listening on an upstairs line. Lauren knew he had a background in covert operations, and she sometimes suspected that he still practiced his skills around the library. He told Barb he had a couple of ideas for halls and then he suggested, "If you've got the bucks, ma'am, the homeless people would love it if you rented a vacation house where they could stay warm and take showers and wash their clothes before the party."

Barb said, "Great idea, and you sound like the man for the job. We don't want any kind of prissy place, not one of those cutesy B and Bs where they put chocolate on the pillows. Maybe you could find the hall and a house for me? Try to get one with three or more bedrooms so I have one, Lee can have one, and other folks can use the other one. So I should get there tonight. Can I meet up with you when I get there around eight or nine?"

Richard said, "Sure, come on by my place when you get into town and I'll tell you what I've found. No, you don't have to give me a credit card number now." He gave Barb directions to his house, hung up, and joined Lauren in the workroom.

"She sounds like quite a character," he said. "I bet it's going to be a party to remember. She wants all the homeless invited, and everyone from the library, and anyone else Billy knew."

"I wonder what she looks like," Lauren said. "She's got to be about fifty, since Billy's birthday cake was for his fiftieth. He told me she's a rancher's wife and I picture her wearing one of those western style shirts with lots of little pearl buttons on the chest pockets."

"I bet she's well endowed, with some cleavage showing where that shirt is unbuttoned, and I'll guess she's plump and has her hair dyed blonde," Richard sad.

"I'll add a lot of makeup and perfume." Lauren's eyes twinkled.

He said, "After I help Barb get things set up tomorrow, I'm going to Denver to get Sunshine. She's been wanting to come visit this weekend."

"I thought she would hate a big party."

"We could only stay a little while before she'd get antsy, but she's been wanting to see you."

"I'd love to see her, too," Lauren said. Richard's close friend Sunshine had wanted to die when they met last year, and Lauren had helped her get beyond that. The circumstances had been bizarre, but all that had passed. It would be good to meet again.

Richard cleared his throat. "I simply have a gut feeling to get her here this weekend."

Lauren said, "I believe in following intuitions. I've got a neighbor, an older lady named Momo, who's been encouraging me to pay more attention to mine."

"Oh, yeah? When I was doing operations overseas, a couple of times a crawling feeling in the back of my neck saved my skin."

"I thought I came in to the library early today to work on the budget, but now I think it was to get this call from Barb," Lauren said, turning back to her computer.

2: BARB

"YOU LOOK TIRED, Richard," Lauren said early Friday morning as she arrived at the library. Richard always began cleaning around six in the morning, but he didn't usually seem at all tired. He tended to project a vibe of being able to handle anything. His crisp black clothing and neck tattoo added to his powerful look, but it was more the way he carried himself, confident and quiet.

"Barb wore me out. She kept going darn near all night."

Lauren looked at him, not following what he meant.

"She got to my place about ten last night, and you know how sometimes the chemistry is just there?"

Lauren began to get a sense of where this was going. Richard didn't talk much about his personal life, but what else could he mean? Lauren had certainly noticed that he was attractive, but she had a great thing going with Justin.

"That lady is one hottie, let me tell you. You'd have to call her a cougar… she must have fifteen years on me. She'll be here after she picks up some coffee, and we can plan Billy's party. Of course, I wouldn't have said anything to you, but I knew she would. She's a talker."

When Barb arrived with three specialty coffees, they settled down in the staff room to plan. Lauren noticed that their guesses as to what she looked like were right on, except Barb's hair was a bright red rather than blonde. Barb engulfed Lauren in a well-perfumed hug and said, "Thank you so much for being there for Billy and Lee. They have had a heck of a life, and you made a difference."

Lauren was still startled by Richard's revelation. But she was happy to tell Barb that she felt public libraries should be open to everyone. She went right into what Justin called her homeless rant. Barb hadn't thought about libraries and the homeless, and she asked several good questions. Lauren could have gotten into a long conversation with her—she hadn't found anyone so interested since she had begun working to make the library more accessible. Often it seemed that most of the library patrons in the town were so indignant about the smells and looks of Billy and his friends that they couldn't see them as fellow human beings.

"What do we need to plan for the party?" Lauren asked.

"Honey, I think Richard and I have it all worked out." Barb winked at Richard and added, "Richard told me the story of Sunshine and what happened in Afghanistan. When I get the chance to talk to that woman, I'm going to tell her she has the love of a good man. I'm going to say Richard is one of the sweetest men around and he would never hurt her. You wouldn't know how gentle a lover he is to look at his tough-guy clothes, would you? I gotta say, he's extraordinary, and you can guess I've been around the block a few times."

Lauren's mouth opened involuntarily. Richard looked down at the floor as if examining it for places in need of mopping. "Let's go over the party plans with Lauren, Barb," he suggested.

He had found a vacation house that was in need of repairs but still usable. He rented it for the weekend, as its private location and four bedrooms made it perfect. It was in a large yard on the edge of town, not far from the river. Access was easy, via back roads that the homeless would feel comfortable coming into town on, whether on foot or in their various old vehicles. The house was only a couple of blocks from an old dance hall that probably should have been condemned by now, but historic preservation people were hoping to restore it. He had managed to rent the hall too. It was right on the river and had sweeping views across the river to fields and mountains beyond.

Barb would go shopping for the food and drink, and she was going to stop by the shelter and the camp where many homeless people lived, and she'd invite them all. She asked Lauren to make and put up a flyer in the library too. Barb said the party would start about eight the next night.

Richard yawned. "Now, if you'll excuse me, I'm going to go home for a nap and then go up to Denver to get Sunshine. Lauren, here is my key. Can you give this to Daniel today when he comes in to do the shelving? I've already told him to do the cleaning tomorrow morning."

"Sure." Lauren was glad she didn't have to say anything else. People could sure amaze you. Richard had surprised her last year, in the weeks after he found Mark Wagner's dead body in the non-fiction stacks, but this was an even more startling side to him.

3: POTLUCK

LAUREN WALKED HOME from the library that evening, through her historic neighborhood full of well-kept yards and old houses painted white or in pleasant colors. She had been lucky to get a cute little old house just three blocks from work, which she bought after she came to Silvermine for the library director's job. She'd lived in the charming old town for a couple of years now. She loved its historic downtown, full of red brick buildings from the mining era that gave the town its name. Many of them had been restored into galleries, shops, and restaurants. The Colorado mountain town had a population of about ten thousand, and Lauren thought it was a perfect size for getting to know people and feeling a sense of community.

Justin had moved in with her last year, not long before he transferred to a Forest Service research position over the mountains in Fort Collins. She missed him, but she liked her independence too. He came home most weekends.

As usual when she walked home, her mind gradually let go of work. Like a child, she kicked fallen leaves on the sidewalks. The weekend was beginning with a family potluck at her house. Justin wouldn't be back from the Front Range till the next day, but his brother Don and Don's wife Betty were coming over, along with their toddler and Betty's grandmother Momo.

Lauren let her little dog Mickey out into the fenced backyard while she set the kitchen table and heated up the chicken soup she'd made. She had been told when she adopted Mickey from a shelter that he was half Sheltie and half Papillon. Weighing about twenty pounds, he was adorable, yappy, and extremely playful.

Betty and Don came in, with Rosie in Don's arms and their Rottweiler Spunky on a leash Betty held. Spunky loved to play with Mickey, despite the size difference. The dogs would wear themselves out playing in the yard. Then Momo arrived, walking across the street. She lived on the other side of the street and down one house, in a house she had owned for decades. Lauren loved having such a lively and wise neighbor. Momo brought a fruit salad for dessert.

As they settled down to eat, Betty dressed a large salad at the table. Her gardening skills were legendary, though the summer's drought and the cold wet autumn had not been easy on many of her plants. Still, the salad included many greens along with fresh tomatoes Betty had been ripening in her basement.

Lauren told everyone about Billy's death. Momo immediately said, "I can feel Billy had a pretty easy passing. He is hanging around Lee and Barb for now, but it seems that what he experienced after death didn't surprise him too much, being a religious guy as he was." Since childhood, both Momo and Betty had had psychic intuitions that came true, sharing a gift that skipped generations. "I feel a kind of amazed joy," Betty added.

Don said, "I knew Billy back when he had a '63 Ford. It was plenty old by then, and I was glad when it gave up the ghost, because Billy was drinking and driving a lot. He was always grateful for my keeping the car going. I remember him as being judgmental of other people. Lauren, what you say about him warning you about a bad man sounds like him."

"What would trigger that, do you remember?" Lauren asked.

"He could get mad at someone and then he would hold a grudge for a while, but because of all his drinking his memory was terrible, so after a while he would forget."

Lauren said, "I'm not going to worry about some bad man coming into the library, even though Billy wanted me to. If it happens, I'll deal with it. Billy's cousin Barb has some great party plans. Can you all come to the party? I've got to tell you, this woman is a hoot. With her being the DJ, the music is going to be from the eighties. Maybe your parents would enjoy coming too. I'll bet they'd enjoy dancing to a lot of those tunes. And it's definitely a party open to everyone."

Momo said, "It sounds like a party I don't want to miss. And I'd be glad to help with Rosie, so long as I can get plenty of dancing in myself!" Momo was in her sixties now, just a little older than Don and Justin's parents, but she was as energetic as anyone.

"Hey, Lauren, otherwise how are things doing at the library?" Don asked.

"With all this rain, we'll have to redo the roof entirely, which will wipe out our emergency funds. I don't know when we'll ever get a new building. I've been hearing lately that people want us to keep the old Carnegie building because it's so darn cute. And I'm afraid my recent outreach to the homeless has been unpopular."

"That doesn't surprise you, does it? After all, people don't want to think about anything unpleasant." Momo softened her remark with a soft laugh.

Lauren said, "But all I'm doing with the homeless is encouraging them to use the library like anyone else. Why should that be such a big deal? It's just fair."

"Lauren the crusader," said Don.

"Look who's talking! You're a crusader for preparedness, Don. Just because you are Justin's baby brother doesn't give you automatic teasing rights," Lauren said.

She glared at him with the well-practiced look that had always stopped her younger brothers from commenting, but Don just said, "Of course it does! Get used to it!" They all laughed.

Don was a couple of years younger than Justin, and despite the teasing he was the more serious of the two brothers. At thirty, Justin had permanent laugh lines around his eyes and radiated a relaxed confidence Lauren found appealing. Both Justin and Don were good looking, tall, athletic in build, and with trimmed beards. It was obvious that they were brothers, even though Don's hair was black and his eyes blue while Justin had brown hair and dark brown eyes.

Lauren had met the Russells soon after she came to Silvermine. She first became friends with Betty, and soon afterwards she met Don and then Justin. She and Justin began hiking together, and their love affair had developed from there. She particularly appreciated that he was comfortable with her intelligence. They had long talks about anything on their minds.

Over dessert, Betty and Don told a few stories of Rosie's latest exploits. Lauren didn't want children herself, as she had grown up with so much responsibility for her five younger siblings that she felt she was done with child raising. Justin didn't want kids because of his concerns about overpopulation. Their agreement was one of many things that made them a good pair.

And it was fun to be around Rosie—in small doses. She quickly tired of sitting at the table, and Don let her down. She would locomote around the house and grab whatever caught her eye. Even though Lauren had Rosie-proofed the house pretty well, Don followed his daughter, just in case, while the rest of them finished eating. Rosie pointed outside to the dogs, and Don let them in. Mickey let Rosie pat him. He cocked his head at the little sounds she made, and Lauren thought he might understand them better than the humans could so far.

"Justin is coming home this weekend, isn't he?" Betty asked.

"Yes," Lauren said. "When we talk tonight, I'll give him a heads up to get ready to boogie." When they went dancing, he loved to go wild.

4: PARTY

THE DANCE HALL had seen better days, so it was perfect for Billy's party. With large parking areas around the old wood frame building, there were no close neighbors to be bothered by loud music. Bruce Springsteen was blaring out as Lauren and Justin walked hand-in-hand up the wide front steps.

They had walked across town from her house, first by the edge of downtown. Then they walked through changing neighborhoods, from her historic one to an area of newer, more nondescript houses built in the forties and later. They had passed close to the highway on the edge of town, dotted with gas stations, motels, fast-food restaurants, big box stores, and the like. Walking a couple of miles through Silvermine might have been a lot of exercise for many people, but not for them. Besides, they could easily catch a ride home with someone if they wanted to. The bright moon helped make it fun to walk.

The large hall was decorated with crepe paper streamers of all colors. Pizzas, vegetable trays from the grocery store, cakes, and other food were loaded on tables along one wall. Along another wall, people were helping themselves to wine, beer, vodka and other hard liquor, orange juice, pop, and steaming coffee from a big urn.

Nobody was dancing yet, but at least fifty people were chatting with each other over the music. Lauren recognized a few of the homeless people as well as some library users. Betty and Don were there, and little Rosie was running around the room at her top speed. Her red knit cap made it easy to track her path, and Lauren noticed quite a few people watching her progress with smiles. Don and Justin's parents were there too, chatting with Momo and some homeless guys.

The Russells had lived in Silvermine for generations, and all of them seemed at home with anyone.

After a while, Barb came out of the kitchen and dropped the volume of the music. She was again wearing a cowgirl style shirt, but this evening it was a richly embroidered two-tone satin with pearl snaps. The shirt was cream and rust, and Barb was wearing it with embroidered rust-colored Western-style boots and cream-colored jeans she was poured into. "I want to thank all of you for coming to give my dear cousin Billy a good sendoff to the next world. I bet he's here with us. And we'll have an out-of-this-world experience ourselves! I know some of you, I've never laid eyes on some of you, and every single one of you is welcome."

Then she said, "I want to thank a couple of people who made this party possible. Richard found the place… is he here? Not yet? Well, give him a hug when he gets here. Lauren at the library was a big help too… she's right there. Lauren, you want to tell everybody what you told me?"

Lauren's practice at Toastmasters came in handy. Smoothly, she said a few words about how the public library was open to everyone, whether or not they had a permanent address, and that she and the staff would be glad to help you learn to use the computers or find a book to read. She went on a bit more, then turned to Barb.

Barb began reminiscing. "Let me tell you about Cousin Billy. He and I grew up together on a ranch in Wyoming, playing together, learning to ride horses together, and getting in all kinds of trouble together. We're the same age but I always looked up to him as the leader. We both managed to finish high school, I'm not sure how, but we did. I was already pregnant with my daughter by then, and right after graduation I married her dad, a cowboy. He and I stayed put and we raised our kids there. We're still there.

"Billy took off, but he'd come back to visit. I noticed after a few years that booze was getting a serious grip on him. He could always have stayed at our ranch or at one of the little rentals I had in town, but he liked life on the road. He would do odd jobs and then move on. And once he came across Silvermine, he liked it best here. As some of you know, he hung out around here for years. He and Lee have been buddies for all those years, and I'm so grateful to Lee." Barb paused as a couple of tears rolled down her cheeks.

She wiped her eyes and continued, "Billy was always the religious one. He'd go to church or more often not go, but he'd always tell me Jesus was around. Now I understand, but back when I was young and foolish I didn't, and Billy kind of kept me on target. Like I said, I was pretty wild, but knowing Billy would be checking up on me kept me from doing a few things I would have regretted."

Barb held up a wooden box of Billy's ashes and asked if anyone could show her where to scatter them the next day. A tall guy said he had an idea for a good place in the forest.

Barb nodded at him and continued, "Billy, you're in Heaven I'm sure, but I know you're also going to party with us right now. And let the good times roll! We've got plenty of food, and if you like your pizza hot there's an oven in the kitchen to warm it up. We have plenty to drink, and a little birdie told me it smelled pot outside, so help yourself to whatever you like and let's dance the night away."

A lively Michael Jackson tune filled the hall, and people started dancing. Lauren and Justin got right into the music, along with the rest of their family. Rosie was bouncing around on her grandpa Pete's shoulders. The homeless people looked good... many of them had been able to get dolled up at the house Richard had rented. Lauren guessed Barb might have given them *carte blanche* at the thrift store.

Lauren saw Margaret Snow, the chair of the library board, doing some wild steps with her husband. Margaret had been a hippie in her early years, and she was dressed the part tonight, in bright ethnic clothing. She and her husband segued into doing the twist. Lauren knew Margaret was a boomer, too young to have done the twist in its heyday, as she was about Momo's age. They had gone to school together. Then Margaret had moved to the Front Range, where she married and worked as a librarian until moving back to Silvermine after an early retirement.

As she looked around the hall, Lauren loved how different kinds of people were having a good time together. The sense of community in Silvermine was a big part of why she had been so happy to get her library job a couple of years ago. Some of this crowd had been drinking steadily, and she smelled the pot wafting in the back door, but whether wigged out or not, everyone seemed cheerful. Barb had set an upbeat tone for sure.

Lauren wondered how many of the crowd were homeless. Billy had told her there were about twenty people who camped out near the bridge, but the Silvermine Homeless Shelter, run by a non-profit and supported by a lot of local churches, took in a larger number, including families and most of the women. Some of the women and kids here were probably from the shelter. Billy and his friends didn't go there much... he'd said it was too small.

Lauren felt a wave of regret for Billy's death wash over her, not just for his sake this time. He'd been a great storyteller, and she'd been getting a sense of what life was like out there near the bridge. She wanted to know more about these people.

Justin snapped his fingers in front of her face, and she realized she had been dancing automatically while she thought. She smiled and brought herself back to the room.

She saw Richard and Sunshine over by the pizzas, snacking as they watched the dancing. Lauren tapped Justin on the shoulder—Barb definitely was playing the music loud—and pointed at them. He followed as she danced over to see them. Sunshine smiled and said something, but Lauren just pointed at her ear and shrugged.

Sunshine pointed at the front door, and Lauren followed her outside onto a porch. "Hey Lauren, thanks again for saving my life last year!" Sunshine said.

"I didn't really," Lauren said, remembering the bizarre nature of their meeting.

"I dunno about that, but I'm doing way better now. I'm selling some of my cross-stitch on etsy, and I'm doing needlepoint mostly now."

"That's great! How are you liking the party?"

"Not much, we'll go soon. But I wanted to come to pay my respects. I didn't know Billy but I've been homeless, and it's so hard." Sunshine looked tough with her muscular build, overalls, work boots, faded shirt, and heavily applied eye makeup, but that was protective coloration. She was a gentle soul.

5: MURDER

LAUREN AND JUSTIN took some pizza slices through the swinging doors to heat them up in the kitchen. Several people were standing around talking near the big institutional stove. It was warmer and less drafty in the kitchen, and the topic was Billy's death.

Barb was saying,, "So what I heard was that Billy was injected with heroin, some of the real strong stuff that's been coming in. Since he'd been drinking as usual, he just stopped breathing pretty quick, and that was the end."

She continued softly, "Whoever killed him might be here, and I just want to say I think whoever did it maybe did it out of compassion. But it upset me so much I can't talk about it without crying. I didn't think it would be Billy's time to go so soon. I wish I could have seen him even one more time. I wish he would have come home and let me take care of him in his last years." She pulled out an embroidered handkerchief and blew her nose vigorously.

Lee said, "He was stubborn about his independence, always. That night I was sleeping right close, but I didn't hear a thing. I woke up in the morning and Billy was already cold, and I saw the needle on the ground." Tears poured down his cheeks, and another guy patted his back and handed him some tissues.

"Sounds like Billy just ODed," an older man said.

"Billy hasn't done drugs, not H anyway, in a good ten years," Barb argued. "He was proud of that. He'd say he was clean but not sober. Then he'd laugh and say he thought he never would get off drinking."

"That's true about the drugs," Lee said. "We hung out together for years and I never saw him shoot up."

The same older man said bluntly, "Well, I'm not going to name any names, but we all know you can get heroin around here cheap. And we know who sells it." He glared at the group as if they were all dealers.

Another guy said, "I'm weirded out by the fancy rock they found by Billy's feet. I guess it had to be put there by the person who took Billy out. But why was the rock there? It spooked me when I saw it. Like somebody was saying something with it. You know, we don't have that kind of rock around here. It's the kind they have in Crestone, where there's all those New Agers and Buddhists and who knows what all. Did one of them come here?"

A young man with dull eyes said, "I want to know who did it. I just want to watch out for them when I'm sleeping out. The cops aren't going to care. I have to protect myself. I ain't ready to go meet Jesus with my sins on my head… I haven't hardly slept since they got Billy." He sure looked like he hadn't slept, Lauren thought.

Barb said, "When I talked to the sheriff's department the other day, they said they didn't have any evidence. The officer said it can be hard to figure out homicides when it's homeless people. There usually aren't many clues. And with the needle there, he said it just looked more like an overdose than anything. I told him Billy didn't use, but he didn't take me seriously. He said the family members often didn't know." She wiped her eyes. "But I know he wasn't using."

Lee said, "Like you said before, Barb, it could have been somebody like me who couldn't bear watching Billy go downhill. Heck, if I'd had the nerve and the smarts, I might have done it myself. But I have no nerves left and you all know my smarts are gone." Lauren thought he still had a big heart.

"I can point to some people," a skinny guy said. "Ace. Garrett. Even you'd be a suspect, Lee. Or the bunch of losers who sleep about a mile from our camp. Maybe the dealer. Or what's her name, that old girlfriend of Billy's. I'm just sayin' we all know someone who might have done it. There could be other ones I haven't thought of, but there aren't that many people around who it could be." He squinted his eyes and looked around. "I'm right, aren't I?"

Lee said, "It wasn't me, man." Nobody else said anything. People looked at the floor or at the walls.

Barb finally said, "Well, we've all got to go sooner or later, and I think Billy has got to be in a much better place now. Let's just leave it at that."

People wandered back into the hall. It was getting chilly, so Lauren and Justin danced to keep warm as much as for the oldies music. She watched a tall, scruffily-bearded guy about her age intimidating some of the young women by dancing right behind their partners and staring at the women. She pointed the scenario out to Justin.

Justin stiffened. "Hey, that's Ace. He did that at high school dances too… He was a year ahead of me. I haven't seen him since he graduated… but it looks like he still has a fondness for intimidating people. His younger brother Garrett is over there drinking. Garret was in Don's class but he dropped out and went in the service before graduation."

Garrett was wearing black clothing with a heavy silver chain, and he had tattoos. It was the kind of look Richard had, but where Richard had flair, Garrett just looked nondescript, his posture bent over, his unkempt hair greasy.

Ace and Garrett… weren't those the first two names that skinny guy had mentioned?

Ace came dancing over to them. It was more bouncing than dancing, but it did provide a rapid form of movement. "If it isn't old Just-in-Time! Haven't seen you in years, fellow. And you've got yourself a librarian?" He ogled Lauren.

"Hey, old Top Nerd," Justin said flatly. "You're still around, huh? This is my girlfriend, Lauren."

"Lauren the Librarian," Ace said. "You got any decent computers at the library, with any speed for surfing?"

"Some," Lauren said. "When you look at the row, the one on the far left is best."

"Good, I'll come see if you folks really do welcome the homeless."

"That's what you've come to, Ace?" Justin asked.

"By choice, totally. You remember I like my freedom. And Mr. Straight Arrow, you'd be interested that I stopped the heavy drinking and hard drugs a while back, when I noticed them interfering with my mind." Ace bounced away.

When the party wrapped up, Barb thanked everyone and said Billy had really been sent off in style. It had rained during the evening, but Lauren and Justin walked home, enjoying the fresh, damp air.

6: SUNDAY

LAUREN AND JUSTIN sat at her kitchen table, waking up with coffee and talking over the party. Mickey was curled up at their feet. "I think it was really great," Lauren said. "I loved seeing everyone having a good time together."

Justin said, "I bet Ace will go to the library. Watch out for him, he can twist your mind around."

"You sound like Billy warning me about the bad man. Do you suppose it was Ace he meant?"

"Well, I don't know. It might have been some other guy from the camp but Ace is a mind-bender all right. He's a tricky guy."

"What about his younger brother? Garrett is the brother's name?"

"Yeah, and I don't think he'll be turning up in the library. He could hardly read in high school. Ace got the brains in that family and it seemed like there weren't any left for Garrett."

"Was Ace as smart as you?"

"Just about. We had a rivalry about that. We competed pretty fiercely… we had math and science classes together since I had been moved up in those subjects. He had always been the smartest kid in those classes and he didn't like it when I came along."

"So that's where those insult nicknames came from?" she asked.

"Yeah, and we had a lot more, mostly pretty offensive. We've always been so different. He was—and obviously still is—a rebel. I was shocked to hear him say he's homeless. He sounds like he hasn't done a thing with his life. Last I knew he was starting at Colorado College, living with relatives in the Springs, and playing poker for money. I heard he was pretty good, and it made sense with his mathematical mind. But now he's a bum, far as I can tell. What a waste."

Lauren asked Justin if he thought Ace could have killed Billy.

"I'll stay out of that without more facts, but Ace always used his mind to be a trickster. He'd go to class totally wasted on pot or whatever and still talk coherently. He had a great memory too. If he didn't kill the guy, I'd say he could have. He never had much in the way of morals. Blatantly stole a girlfriend away from me one time."

Lauren thought to herself, "Aha."

"The only thing I can say in his favor is that he was protective of Garrett. The poor kid took a lot of teasing for being different. Ace told off some of those kids and beat up a couple of the worst ones. Don probably remembers that."

Lauren petted Mickey absently as she said, "Intense family."

Justin said, "Don't waste your time talking to Ace if he goes to the library."

"I don't need you telling me who I can talk to," Lauren said. She couldn't resist a small barb and went on, "Particularly if they are smart."

Justin frowned. He could be sensitive and he rarely missed her nuances. He immediately retaliated, "Now that Billy's party is over, you should get over your obsession with the homeless."

"Obsession!"

"Yes, or are you going to be the super-sleuth who solves the riddle of Billy's murder? If that's what it was?"

Lauren took a deep breath. It was true that she had thought she might figure out who did the killing.

Justin went on, "If you want a real purpose beyond your library work, it's obvious it should be the environment. You know nothing else matters if we can't save the planet."

"Justin, I know how important that is to you, but I see all the issues of the world as inter-connected. I think that's why being a librarian suits me. I'm researching homelessness now, and another time it might be carbon footprints, and another time eating vegan."

"Vegan! You mean without any meat at all? I wouldn't like that," Justin said. "I know the environmental issues but I still like my grass-fed steak or other healthy meats in moderation."

"Well, I haven't done any research on that one yet, so do you want to fry up the turkey bacon while I turn out some gluten-free waffles?"

Over breakfast, Justin said, "I'm not sure this is the greatest time to tell you, but I've already talked with my family and I don't see waiting or telling you over the phone…"

"Let's get it over with," she said. Justin had an annoying way of building up to telling bad news, she thought.

"I'm over halfway through my assignment to the Rocky Mountain Research Station in Fort Collins, as you know…"

"Yep, been counting the months till you come back to Silvermine full time next year."

Justin stared at his plate as he said, "I'm not sure if I want to come back. I really like the work I'm doing there, and the research libraries and connections on the Front Range are far beyond what Silvermine has. Frankly, my old Forest Service job here is something anybody can do, and I feel like the research I'm doing now is far more likely to make a difference in the world."

Lauren nodded. "I do understand, honey. I really know how important it is to you. So do you want to break up with me?" She could hardly breathe as she asked, but she couldn't bear not knowing the truth.

"No! Why do you say that? I want to marry you and do the happily-ever-after bit." He glanced at her with a small smile.

"You want to have a long-distance marriage? I don't. You know that's why I wouldn't marry you when you asked me last year. Have you forgotten?"

"Lauren, be reasonable," Justin said, his voice rising. "There are lots of libraries where you could work, within about an hour's drive of Fort Collins. Some of them are in cute little towns. We could wait till you got a job to decide where to buy a house, so neither one of us would have that bad of a commute."

"I can't believe I'm hearing you say this," she said. "I thought you loved Silvermine like I do. How well do I know you, Justin? Sounds like I had stars in my eyes when I fell in love with you, thinking you were as rooted in Silvermine as I wanted to be." She thought to herself that she sounded like someone in a soap opera, but she meant it all.

He tried a little levity. "Maybe you confused me with Don on that one. I don't think you could get him out of here. But honey, we could keep this house and take vacations back here."

"Look," she said in exasperation, as Mickey ran back and forth between their feet, his little face looking up anxiously as the argument went on. She tried to pick the dog up, but he was too agitated to sit still. "I am the director of the Silvermine Public Library. They hired me to spearhead a movement to improve services and to get a much better building. I've improved a lot of services, and I've told you about every single thing as it's happened. We have had setbacks about the idea of a new building, and the old one is leaking like a sieve. This is my work. It matters a lot to me." She couldn't help glaring at him.

She went on, not giving him a chance to break in, "Living here in Silvermine, I finally feel like I belong somewhere. You grew up here and you seem to take it for granted, Justin, but I grew up in dingy apartments all over the Front Range, and I never had a sense of belonging to any community. But here, every project I've done for the library, even every time I've helped someone find a book, I've felt I was weaving connections that could last my lifetime. Sure, I know that lots of librarians move around, and lots of them choose their new jobs by the size of the paychecks. That isn't me. I love Silvermine and I am not going to give it up!" She looked out the window at her back yard and thought how much she loved her home.

"We're obviously at an impasse," he said. "Let's drop the subject. How about if we take Mickey for a walk in the park and just chill?"

"That's the first thing you've said that makes sense," she said. "Let's end up at the latte place."

A brisk wind was blowing down the few leaves remaining on the cottonwoods by the river. They walked quickly, hand in hand, while Mickey ran out to the end of his leash in one direction and then another. He had a great time, but Lauren couldn't help feeling that the difference between what she wanted and what Justin wanted was too great. This walk was not at all like the many happy times they had taken the same route, lattes and all.

Later, they made love, but even that felt poignant. Had a dream been shattered?

7: CONVERSATIONS

EARLY MONDAY MORNING, Barb came by the library to say goodbye to Lauren and Richard. She told Lauren that she had met Sunshine.

"I told her she was never goin' to find a better man than Richard and it would be a durn shame to go the rest of her life without a lover just because of what happened to her once. She'd be missing out on such a beautiful part of life. I told her to go get in bed with him, with an agreement they would just cuddle the first week. After that, she should just let things develop, but she should be the one calling the shots. And I guess it helped, because then I didn't see them much."

"Thanks so much, Barb, Sunshine is feeling better." Richard didn't volunteer any intimate details but he did say, "I think that little talk with you was why I had a feeling to bring her to Silvermine this weekend."

"Well, Richard, I'm glad to help. It was a pleasure and you've got my cellphone number so let's keep in touch." Richard gave Barb a quick goodbye hug, and went upstairs to continue the cleaning.

Barb said to Lauren, "Lee and Ace and some others took me out in the woods and we buried Billy's ashes. We sang a nice song for Billy there too. You probably know it, 'In the Sweet Bye and Bye.' I felt completely at peace about Billy's passing after we sang to him."

Barb went on, "That Ace has an amazing mind, real brilliant. After we buried the ashes, I took him out for a steak dinner. We talked a lot about homelessness and why it exists. I talked with him about some ideas for a memorial for Billy that could help out here, but I can't tell you anything yet, gotta talk to my old man at home. He's a pretty generous guy and he loved Billy too."

Lauren wondered if her husband knew how generous Barb could be with her body. As if she sensed what Lauren was thinking, Barb said, "Too bad he can't do it anymore, but he makes it up to me in other ways. By the way, I'm going to mail a cellphone to Lee, all set up and paid for, to the library if that's okay with you, so I can stay in better touch with him. Well, I gotta get on home."

During the afternoon, Lee came into the library, looking ill at ease. He mumbled an apology for interrupting Lauren, and she said, "I was just about to fall asleep over some work. Would you like to come downstairs to the office, and we can talk a little?"

"Can we send Barb another email?"

"Sure, we can do that from the computer there."

So they settled down and he dictated a flowery, polite thank-you to Barb for everything she had done. "She's a rare woman," he said to Lauren. "The first time I went to the ranch with Billy, I was kinda worried how she would take to me, you know… with me not being white. Barb never cared one bit, and she's helped me out with money and kindness. I thought she threw a great party this weekend."

Lauren agreed and said she didn't care about race either.

"Oh, I know you don't. Believe me, I can tell right away when I'm around someone. Billy never cared. I miss him so much. I'll never have as good a friend as Billy, I don't think. He and I always looked out for each other. I been trying to imagine what it's like where he is, you know, in Heaven. All I can imagine is that he isn't cold or hungry or hurting. That sounds good to me."

Lauren said, "My neighbor—she's like an aunt to me—Momo can see the next world, and she said Billy had a pretty good passing and he wasn't too surprised at what it was like, being as religious as he was."

Lee nodded. "Thank you kindly for telling me that. It's a real comfort." More tears flowed, and Lee got up to go. "I have to be a friend to some of the other guys out there, Garrett and them. There are several who lean on me. It makes me try to keep up my faith, so I can help them a little."

"I'm glad you are there for them," Lauren said. "By the way, have you had any more ideas who Billy might have been calling a bad man?"

"Oh, he'd rag on someone for a while and then forget about it. Since you told me he mentioned a brother, I guess he meant Garrett or Ace, since they're the only brothers there. They sure are both plenty different." Lee chuckled, and then he walked out abruptly. It had flickered through Lauren's mind to ask him if he thought one of them had killed Billy. She guessed Lee might have sensed her question and left to avoid answering it.

*****

At the Russell family potluck Monday evening, held at the ranch of Justin and Don's parents, Lauren felt awkward about being there since she didn't know what would happen with her and Justin. Things eased when Sue, Justin's mother, said to Lauren, "Justin told us he's thinking of staying in Fort Collins. He said you weren't happy about it."

Lauren blinked to keep the tears from coming. "Nope."

"Well, we don't have to talk about it if you don't want to, but I just want to say we all consider you family no matter what you and Justin do."

"Thanks," Lauren said. She couldn't say more without crying.

Betty started a story about Rosie's antics, to get off the painful topic.

As Lauren drove Momo home after the potluck, she told Momo about her conversation with Justin. "I've had such trouble finding men smart enough to hold my interest, and I really thought Justin was going to be the one, but maybe I was wrong."

"Easy, honey," Momo said. "Let me do a little visioning as we drive."

She closed her eyes and Lauren heard her let out a long breath. Then Momo was silent for a while, and then she murmured, "Ahhhhh."

She said, "Lauren, it's not like I'm reading a novel and I skipped ahead in the book to see what happens. It's not that certain… it's more changeable depending on what you and Justin do going forward. But I did see the auras of the two of you intertwined. I saw colors, green mainly for him, and gold for you, and they were in a spiral like a cinnamon cookie."

"That helps," Lauren said. "We'll have to wait and see. Between Justin and everything going on around the library, I'm overwhelmed."

"Remember to breathe," Momo said. "I mean it. It helps a lot."

8: REFLECTIONS

ONE AFTERNOON AT the library, Lauren discovered they had no books on homelessness. Grace volunteered to find a few recent titles to buy. "I know there is one called *How to Shit in the Woods*, meant for campers."

Lauren giggled at the title. "Probably most of the homeless are experts on that particular subject, but it sounds like a good one to have for campers anyway."

Grace said, "Paul and I have been talking with the kids about homelessness since Billy died. When Paul was on the police force in D.C., he had to deal with homeless people all the time. Out here in Silvermine, not so much. For one thing, the cold and the snow we get here mean it's not exactly a magnet for homeless people. When Paul had the chance to get a job in the Silvermine police department, we both thought it would be good for the kids to live in such a peaceful place."

"You still think it was a good choice?" Lauren asked.

Grace said, "Yes, absolutely. Our kids are all teenagers now, you know, and they are away from big-city temptations. Sure, there are some kids offering them pot and heavier stuff but they've made friends we approve of, and they love to ski." Grace was a devoted mother, now in her early forties. Lauren had seen her being fiercely protective of her children when the family first arrived and the kids received some racist taunts from white students.

Grace continued reflecting. "Paul was telling me how law enforcement gets caught in the middle between the average citizen's desire for the homeless to just disappear and the need to respect the rights of the homeless. People get scared by panhandling, but it's legal in a lot of places."

Lauren said, "That makes a lot of sense to me, what you say about getting caught in the middle. I feel that way myself here when people get mad at me for letting homeless people use the library."

Grace said, "By the way, I asked Paul if he thought law enforcement would find out who killed Billy. In a nutshell, Paul said they didn't have any clues. Since it could been an overdose that Billy administered himself, they are basically letting it ride in case something new comes up."

"That's what the sheriff's deputy told Barb," Lauren said. "I wonder who Billy was trying to warn me about when he talked about a bad man. It seems Ace has a reputation for being a bad guy."

"It's just talk." Grace changed the subject. "Say, what shall we do for the Halloween program for the kids? I'd sure like to get away from providing sugary snacks."

"I bet you'll be good at telling scary stories, Grace," Lauren said. "I agree with you… it would be good to stay away from treats. The kids will get more than enough of those anyway. Want to do different stories for different age groups?"

*****

Lauren heated up some leftovers for dinner. She ate them on the sofa, Mickey curled up beside her with his little head resting on her thigh. He looked like he was relaxing but she knew he would move at the speed of light if anything fell off her plate. She liked having him there as she reflected on her life. Was she obsessed with the homeless, as Justin had said? Nobody minded when she threw her curiosity into needlepoint or recipes, but her interest in making the library available to homeless people bothered a lot of people.

But if you can't keep your heart open to the sufferings of others, how can you be authentic in these times? She didn't want to be like the nicey-nice people who ignored everything they didn't want to recognize.

She remembered a quote from the Dalai Lama. A reporter had asked him how he could laugh so much and be so joyous when the world was so full of terrible events. The Dalai Lama had laughed and said, "What else do you suggest?"

Lauren thought she could make a deliberate effort to be more joyous. Well, Justin had brought her a lot of joy, but not right now. Maybe she needed a hobby. She had loved photography all her life. She immediately saw in her mind's eye a series of black and white photographs, portraits of Lee. A few of those would go great with the book display on homelessness that she and Grace were planning when the books they had ordered came in.

She could do plenty of other things with photography too. She thought of doing photos of Mickey playing with Spunky, thinking that would challenge her skills as the dogs moved around so fast. But nature would provide a lot of opportunities that stayed still, more or less, such as trees.

Lauren got her camera out and began playing with its settings.

9: ACE

ACE CAME INTO the library on a rainy evening. Lauren was working the evening shift, and it took her a moment to recognize him. He was almost as tall as Justin, but he stood with a bit of a slouch. He had red-brown curly hair tied back loosely into a pony tail. His unkempt beard was redder than his hair. It wasn't long, and it looked like he carelessly snipped it with scissors now and then. Ace had freckles she hadn't noticed at the party. Once he placed his rain hat and jacket on the library coat rack, she saw he had on jeans and a nondescript plaid shirt. Actually, she thought to herself, there was nothing about him that would make it evident that he was homeless. A lot of graduate students looked much the same.

She showed Ace the fastest computer, and he asked her for a tour of the place.

"Well, it won't take long. We have the fiction over there, where you can see the magazines by those lounge chairs. The non-fiction is on the other side of the room. The circulation desk is opposite the front door, and the reference desk is where I was sitting when you came in. Then downstairs, we have the children's section, the staff workroom, and the bathrooms. Didn't you use this library when you were a child?"

"Yeah, but that was a long time ago. Hey, I'm older than Justin."

"Well, it's hardly changed since then. I carved out the staff room downstairs from a corner of the children's section and we moved things around a little upstairs, but the building is the same size as it was back then. It's really inadequate for a town this size."

Ace said, "I bet you make people talk quietly and watch their language, like the old lady librarians when I was a kid here."

Lauren said, "No, public libraries have changed a lot about being quiet. We don't want people yelling, of course, but talking in normal tones is fine. If someone is swearing in a carrying tone of voice, I ask them not to."

"Lauren the Librarian," he said. "People who swear a lot are inarticulate. But I want to know, why did you take the job since the library is so bad?"

"We're hoping to get a new building, and the board hired me to spearhead the campaign. I'm working on it, but it's not easy."

"Money," he said. "That's all. Just play poker."

Lauren snorted and stepped back. Ace had moved closer to her as they talked, and she thought of how he had moved in on women at Billy's party. Lauren had had an Algerian friend in college who stood extremely close, but he had explained that it was normal in his culture. Ace was no Algerian.

"So you went to DU," he said. "CC is much better."

"I'm surprised to hear you getting into that stale competition," she said. "I went to DU because I lived in Denver, and then I got my Master's in Library and Information Science there because it's a good school and I could keep on living at home."

"Just wondered what you'd say. I only went to Colorado College for two years before I'd had enough of it."

They sat down in a couple of the lounge chairs and Lauren blurted out, "Well, I'll tell you what I wondered. Why are you homeless?"

"Look, what we all have is our lives. That means our time. If I had an apartment or a house, I would be paying money, and I'd have to waste time working to get it. So it isn't worth it to me. I could live with my relatives—they're mostly in Colorado Springs now—and sometimes I stop by, but I can only stand a short time with them before I remember what dysfunctional means."

"But isn't it hard to have no place?"

"I have a funky old van where I keep stuff, and I usually sleep in it.

I don't tell most people where it's parked, and I move it around. I have several places to park it, some pretty public like in the Walmart parking lot, others way back in the woods, and some in between. Don's worked on it quite a few times. I keep it in running condition—that gives me the freedom to take off any time I want. So you could say that I'm not exactly homeless, I'm just into the RV lifestyle."

She laughed at the way he put it. "If you don't mind my asking, what do you do for money?"

"I don't need much. I work now and then… odd jobs or whatever, and I like farm labor. It's straightforward. I work around here, or down in New Mexico. I can scavenge food by dumpster diving or I go to the food banks, and I know people at restaurants who will give me leftovers late at night, when they close. I used to play poker for money. I can always go into some low-stakes games in a casino, where most of the people are idiots, and make enough for it to be worth my time."

Lauren was glad that nobody was nearby, likely to overhear them.

Ace said, "I like talking with you, because you're plenty smart. You could probably understand how society is really set up if you haven't been too brainwashed. I always prefer to talk at more complex levels, but there aren't many people who can follow what I say." Lauren thought to herself that he was plenty arrogant, and that he was enjoying this all the more because she was Justin's girlfriend.

His mind must have turned to Justin also. "Don't worry, I won't come on to you. Since you're Justin's girlfriend, if you slept with me, you'd be messed up about it. Of course, I think being messed up is often a good thing—it can be the only way for new ideas to come in—but I'm done with younger women."

Lauren thought Ace's comments were the verbal equivalent to the way he had been standing so close. But her curiosity led her to ask, "So you don't have girlfriends?"

"No, I have women friends. I go for older women who have been around long enough to realize they aren't going to save me from homelessness, have kids with me, be rescued by me, or run any of the other agendas young women get off on. Give me a cougar anytime. I have lady friends I visit now and then. I turn up, see if it's cool, hang out for a day or two if it is, then take off again."

Ace said, "One older woman who's just a friend is Barb. She understands the whole homeless thing really well because of Billy, but he was an example of the old-timer homeless guy who could hardly keep it together. I updated her on how this country simply doesn't have enough affordable housing, and that there are a lot of people who've had a couple of whacks of bad luck and then they find themselves out on the street. She's a smart woman, but she didn't understand some things about politics and economics I explained. But hey, Wyoming is mostly white and conservative, so I don't think she'd been exposed to my kind of ideas much before."

The library would be closing in a few minutes, and Lauren needed to start the closing routines. But would she ever get another chance to talk to Ace like this?

"Who do you think killed Billy?" she asked.

"I don't think it matters, but several of the guys who camp out there, by the bridge or up the hill, could have done it. Maybe Billy asked for some heroin, and it was really an assisted suicide. I doubt Lee could have put the needle in him, though. Maybe my brother was involved. He could have done it. Serving overseas in the military messed up what was left of his mind. I didn't kill Billy. I wouldn't because I have seen some of my own past lives and I don't want the karma of a killing on me. But if I had killed the poor guy, I would lie to you and say I hadn't."

"That's quite a string of thoughts," she said. "Specially that last one. Are you the guy Billy called the bad man?"

"Some people call me the adversary, since I argue with them. It hasn't escaped my attention that 'the adversary' is also a name for the devil. Maybe I should take that as a compliment, but since I don't believe in good and evil, I don't see myself as evil incarnate!" He guffawed, and Lauren thought you could call it an evil laugh.

10: OKAY

ACE CAME TO the library on another rainy evening and used the fastest computer for a while. Then he said he wanted to talk with her. Lauren put enough extra hours into her work that she never minded taking time to talk with a library patron. She sat down next to where he was sitting at the computer. The library was practically empty and nobody was within earshot.

"I'm a trickster by nature," he confided.

"Yes, Justin called you that," she said.

Ace frowned. Then he said, "Here's a definition of trickster consciousness that I found online: 'an openness to life's multiplicity and paradoxes largely missing in the modern Euro-American moral tradition.' That fits me perfectly."

She nodded. It did fit him, and it was why she found him interesting. Fascinating, even. She'd been wondering what he meant when he said she might be able to understand how society was set up. She'd been insulted when he said that, but now she wanted to know more. Would he go into secret international cabals, or what?

"People love their boxes," he said. "Everyone likes to have a soapbox they can stand on and be right. I don't mean right-wing, though there are plenty of nut cases in that group… but you will find people who need to be right in every group, in every church, and believe me, there are tons of them among lefties and do-gooders."

"I can't really argue with that," Lauren said. "It seems to be part of how human minds work."

He snorted. "Humans are idiots. But you know that expression that people use all the time, 'thinking outside the box?'"

She nodded.

"What people don't want to see is that there is no box." He leaned back in his chair, with a grin of satisfaction on his face, as he watched her face.

Lauren thought she had an idea what he meant, but she wasn't sure. "No box?"

"What do you suppose I mean by that?" he asked with a smirk.

"Let's see, no DU versus CC, no Christians versus Muslims or atheists, and so on. That is, we all use labels that don't really mean much… I feel like I'm back in college with a philosophy professor nailing my mind."

"That was one possible career path for me," he said. "I did consider it. But let's go on. When people say someone thinks outside the box, they are talking about the box as consensual reality, and implicit in that is the idea the box is real. Not only is the box real, it's the correct—or at least the normal—way to think. But now, more and more people use the term 'outside the box' in an approving way, because the world is falling apart so much that the boxes are too."

She nodded again. It made sense to her.

He went on, "I'm sure you know the great Yeats poem, *The Second Coming*. My favorite lines are 'Things fall apart; the centre cannot hold… The best lack all conviction, while the worst are full of passionate intensity.' Gotta love that poem. That explains a lot about why I'm not working at a J-O-B like you or Justin. I lack conviction."

"And you're among the best?" she asked.

"I've got one of the best minds, yes."

Lauren didn't think that made him one of the best people but she just said, "Here's a quote I like, from Solzhenitsyn, *The Gulag Archipelago*: 'The line between good and evil runs through every human heart.' It seems to me that complements the Yeats one."

"Ah, but Lauren, do you really believe in good and evil? That's such a simplistic duality."

"Yes, I do," she said. "It may be simplistic but I feel that I have an internal compass that points me towards the good. Sometimes it swings around toward the other side, but it doesn't generally linger there."

"Okay... here's a question for your good and bad mind. It's pouring like crazy outside. You are about to close up the library for the night. My van is parked a couple of miles from here. Wouldn't it be good for you to let me sleep on the floor of the library, on the carpet? What harm would it do? I could leave before you open in the morning."

Lauren started to say no automatically, but then she thought of the old song sung by Pete Seeger, *Which Side Are You On?* It was a union song, and it was about standing up for what you believed in. She believed nobody should have to be homeless on a cold rainy night. She always wanted to alleviate the sufferings of the downtrodden and oppressed. Maybe she could let Ace sleep in the library, just for tonight.

She said okay.

11: FURIOUS

IN THE MORNING, Margaret Snow phoned the library and demanded to speak with Lauren. She was furious. "About three this morning, a police officer driving by the library saw a man sitting in front of a computer. The officer knocked on the door, and it was a homeless man who opened it and said you had let him stay overnight. Is this true?"

"Yes," Lauren said.

"You must know that you were overstepping the bounds of your position. You could let him sleep in your own house or even your own bed, and it would be none of our business, but this is the library. I have called a board meeting which you are not invited to attend. It will be an executive session to discuss personnel matters. We will use the staff room at eleven this morning, and immediately following it we will want to talk with you."

"Okay," Lauren said.

Her stomach was tied up in knots. The board members greeted her, politely but distantly, as they came in and went downstairs. Grace wasn't due to come to work till noon, but Lauren knew she wouldn't get any sympathy there. She didn't know what she had been thinking last night. It was pretty dumb to have jeopardized… what? She'd know soon.

Her fingers shook as she dialed her cellphone, calling Justin to tell him what had happened. He was always so steadfast when she needed him. He reacted immediately to her story. "You did what? I warned you he could twist your mind around. Why didn't you believe me?"

"Thanks for nothing," she said.

All too soon, Virginia Wagner, one of the board members, came upstairs to the reference desk, and said, "Lauren, please join us in the staff room now."

Her heart pounding, she followed Virginia downstairs. The board members were all there, and they didn't look happy.

"Would you tell us what happened, from your point of view?" Margaret asked.

"Well, it was raining hard yesterday evening, and I knew Ace pretty well, so when he asked me if he could sleep on the library floor until Richard came to work, I impulsively said yes."

"Impulsively isn't how we want the Silvermine Public Library run," Margaret said. "We are disappointed that this has happened, and we are putting you on probation for six months. If there are no more incidents, at the end of that time the probation and the cause for it will be expunged from your personnel records. We will all keep our mouths shut about this incident, so it shouldn't be gossiped about if you keep quiet too. But if there are any further problems, we will ask you to resign."

"There won't be further problems," Lauren said, relieved it wasn't worse. "And I have some new ideas for moving forward towards a new building. We can talk about them at our regular meeting next week."

Margaret let out a long breath, and Lauren realized this had been hard on her too. "I'm glad to hear that," Margaret said, and she almost smiled at Lauren. But not quite.

*****

Lauren called Justin that evening, and he was still upset. "Tell me why you let Ace sleep in the library," he said.

"The weather was really bad, and when he asked, it just seemed like a small thing I could do."

"Why? To be the noble one who could relieve suffering?"

She admitted to herself that it was true, but she couldn't quite say that to Justin.

"Well…"

"Well, what? Lauren, how could you not see that he was manipulating you? He loves to play power games. You played right into his scheme. He didn't have to go to the library last night at all. He could have been dry in his van or someplace before it started raining. But he thought it would be more fun to see what he could pull over on you. I bet you he went to the library with the plan in mind to talk you into letting him stay."

"I guess he could have," she said. "That does make sense."

Justin went on, "There's a rebellion in him that isn't likely to change, just as my desire to make something of my life is not going to change. Even though what I do in the future might change, I expect I'll always be trying to do something that helps the environment. Like sometimes I think of farming with Dad, but that's not something to focus on anytime soon. I haven't even mentioned it to you, not wanting to get your hopes up that I'd be in Silvermine."

"That would be cool, if it ever worked out," she said. "It's a way we could endure being a couple and living apart for a while longer."

"I shouldn't have mentioned it. I haven't talked with my parents about the idea lately. But I want you to get this about Ace: he simply doesn't see that the structures that exist in society can be beneficial. Not even libraries or the Forest Service. He's just too locked into being the rebel."

"I guess so," she said.

Justin continued, "And honey, it seems you've gotten sidetracked with the homeless. Do you forget you were hired because of your unique vision for a new library?"

Lauren said, "You sound like a library board member."

Justin said, "Well, don't you need to hear it? And don't forget, curious can also mean prying or meddlesome."

In a low voice she said, "I don't think I am prying or meddlesome."

He let his breath out. "You need more balance at times. I like to think I provide you with some stability, but it's hard when I'm not there and Ace's mind is so flashy."

"Don't talk down to me," she snapped.

"Lauren, I didn't! You provide me with stability too… I wish you were here with me right now." She could hear the pain in his voice.

He continued, "But I just don't trust Ace…"

"He doesn't turn me on, at least," Lauren said.

"Well, that's a relief," Justin said. "Hey, you want to come to Fort Collins with Don and Betty this weekend?"

"I'm not sure," she said. "You and I wouldn't have time alone in your apartment, not with them there. I think I'd rather stay home and do photography and just kick back. It's been so stressful."

"When can I see you, then?" he asked.

"You're coming home the next weekend, right?"

"Yeah, can't wait. Take care, sweetie, we'll get through all this somehow," he said.

On Saturday night at home, Lauren wondered how other librarians were dealing with homeless people. Going online with her laptop on the kitchen table, she found that some libraries had passed policies that effectively kept them out. On the other hand, others were reaching out as she was trying to. San Francisco Public Library had some innovative programs to help them. Lauren was moved by a comment from a newly homeless man who appreciated being able to use that library. He said, "It's very crazy out there, and it's very sane in here."

Lauren saw that because libraries were one of the few public spaces where homeless people could doze off or try to clean themselves up in the bathrooms, if a library didn't allow those activities, it was further marginalizing the poorest, even if inadvertently.

None of the issues were simple, but at least she was comforted that many librarians were struggling with the same questions. And she picked up some new ideas of what she could say to library patrons who complained about homeless people. For one thing, she could quote the Americans with Disabilities Act. Quite a few of the homeless fell under its protection, theoretically at least.

Silvermine wasn't a poor town by any means. There wasn't any mining nowadays, but the downtown did appeal to a lot of tourists. Retirees, the hospital, the university, the outdoors activities—all contributed to make it a thriving town. Lauren had thought about these sources as providing possible income for a new building but now she thought that she really should be able to fund some ways the library could help the homeless soon. Provided she kept her job!

12: ANOTHER

AT THE FAMILY potluck on Monday night, Don told Lauren about their visit to Justin in Fort Collins. "We went out to dinner and had a good time," Don said. "Then we dropped Betty off at Justin's apartment to put Rosie to bed, and Justin and I went out for a beer at a bar down the street."

Don looked at Betty. "Should I tell her the rest, hon?"

Lauren said, "Yes, whatever it is, tell me."

"Well, it's not that bad but it did surprise me. At the bar, who should turn up but his girlfriend from when he was in college there. What was her name… I never knew what her appeal was, but she sure was putting the make on him. She was all over him."

Lauren frowned. "He told me about her when we first got together. All I remember is that he said she was good in bed and otherwise boring. How was he reacting to her?"

"He wasn't pushing her away," Don said. "But he didn't encourage her either. I think he was embarrassed when she sat on his lap, but he was too polite to tell her to get lost."

Lauren felt a primal impulse to get even, but who could she get anything going with? There was an attractive single father who brought his boys to the library story hours. He had talked with her in a flirtatious manner a couple of times, but she didn't want to get involved with a man with children. There was Richard, but he and Sunshine were tight these days. Ace? Nope, he was so weird and besides she just wasn't attracted to him. Also, that would totally push Justin's buttons and he'd probably split up with her permanently. Really, she just wanted things to be good again with Justin.

*****

Lauren's slacks were too tight. She could barely squeeze into them for work. Had she run them through the dryer on too high a setting? No, ever since she and Justin had added the greenhouse on the south side of her house, she had been drying her clothes on the clotheslines in it.

She must be gaining weight. Self-medicating with chocolate must have gotten out of hand. Sure, her stress levels had been really high, but she hated gaining weight. With Justin living away most of the time, she hadn't been hiking as much. With the days getting shorter and all the rain, she wasn't even walking Mickey as much. She hadn't been eating as well, either, another part of the stress reaction.

She went right to the phone. "Carole! Remember we were going to play tennis? Let's do it! I'm gaining weight!"

Lauren's friend Carole was the realtor who had sold Lauren her house, and they often did things together. Carole said, "Sure, how about in the morning? Most of my appointments are later in the day."

"I go to work at noon tomorrow, so how about we meet at nine at the tennis courts in the park?" Lauren said. "My life has gone downhill since I've seen you. I can tell you a different tale of woe every time I win a game. Believe me, I've got enough tales for several sets!"

"That bad, huh?" Carole said. "Of course I want to hear your news, but if you're fat and depressed, I'll beat you easily."

"Don't count on it, girl friend! I'm determined to run down every ball."

By the end of their match the next morning, Carole had heard about the homeless using the library and about Justin thinking of staying in Fort Collins. She'd heard about the old girlfriend wrapping herself around Justin. Lauren had told her about Ace, but she deliberately left out the part of how she ended up on probation at the library. As for the match, Lauren just barely managed to beat Carole, but Carole promised revenge the next week.

"You said you're going to give up chocolate, but you don't really have to," Carole said.

"Oh, you want me to eat it all week so you can beat me?"

"No, Lauren, I'll beat you anyway. But here's what I do, and it's really simple. I heat half a cup of coconut oil so it's liquid… in the summer, I don't even have to do that as it liquifies at seventy-six degrees. Then I add a quarter of a cup of raw cocoa powder, a dash of vanilla, a tiny bit of salt, and a sweetener to taste but not too much. For the sweetener, I use about two tablespoons of honey or maple syrup, but if you're being really pure, I guess you could use stevia."

Carole went on, "I put the mix into ice cube trays and keep it in my freezer. It's healthier than chocolate bars you can buy, since all the ingredients are better. I get my fixings at the health food store. It's satisfying in really small amounts."

"I'll try it," Lauren said. "I'm not wild about stevia's flavor but mixed with chocolate, I think it would be okay."

As they walked through the park, a young woman smoking under the trees called out to Lauren. "Hey, aren't you the library lady who was at Billy's party?"

Lauren turned. She recognized the woman but had only seen her that one time. "Yes, I am. Want to come by the library?"

"I don't read much, but seeing you, I just wondered if you knew that a woman died the same way Billy had, out near the bridge, a couple of days ago."

"No, I hadn't heard anything about it. What do you mean, the same way?"

"She was sleeping in a tent near the bridge and one night a shot of heroin took her out after she'd been drinking. And it was weird, there was one of those pretty rocks at her feet too."

"Who was it?" Lauren asked.

"You wouldn't know her... she didn't leave the camp, because she had breast cancer and just lay around in her tent. We were taking care of her, you know, bringing her food and stuff, and keeping her full of drugs so she didn't have too much pain. Her name was Sylvia, and she was about forty."

"I'm sorry to hear that," Lauren said.

"Yeah, the sheriff took her body and the syringe and stuff. People are saying we've got a serial killer on the loose. I sleep at the shelter anyway, and some of the folks who usually are out at the camp have been coming in."

Lauren said, "Thanks for letting me know, and do come by the library any time you want to."

As she and Carole walked on to the coffee shop, Carole said, "That was intense."

"Just another day in the life." Lauren tried to smile. She couldn't get the conversation off her mind, though. How sad, even if it did sound almost like a mercy killing, if there was such a thing. Having advanced cancer out in the woods with winter coming on sounded grim.

13: CAMP

THE HOMELESS CAMP wasn't far from town, but you had to know which winding roads to take, ending on a narrow gravel one. Justin had been there a few times when he worked out of the Silvermine office of the Forest Service, and he told Lauren the route.

She'd made a date to meet Ace there at nine in the morning so she could see the camp. She had brought some inexpensive sleeping bags to give people there, partly as an excuse for being there.

She parked on the side of the road near where a highway bridge passed high overhead. Would she need to watch her step to avoid garbage or even human excrement? She had worn an old pair of walking shoes. Come to think of it, she had worn only old clothing: jeans, sweatshirt, and jacket.

She left the sleeping bags in the car and set out, Mickey in her arms. There was a trail from the road, easy walking and not particularly dirty. Ace was nowhere to be seen, but she couldn't wait around for him. She stayed on the trail, and it took her to a cleared area in the woods, where a small fire was burning. A few people were sitting on logs and old camping chairs, close to the fire, which had a large enamel coffee pot dangling over it.

"It's the librarian," one of the men said, waving at her. "What's up?"

Suddenly Lauren felt self-conscious. What made her think she would be welcome here? Nobody had invited her. She was just barging into their home.

"Hi, just thought I'd come by and see how things were going," she said. "I was sorry to hear about Sylvia."

The same guy replied. "Bummer. Say, that's a mighty cute little dog you got there. C'mere, little guy… come to Jimbo…"

Lauren let Mickey down and he ran over to Jimbo but darted back when the guy reached out quickly towards him.

"Try it a little slower and he'll come to you. He's cautious with men he doesn't know," she said.

"Here, doggy, doggy, here's a little bit of bread," the guy said, holding it up. Mickey was a sucker for food, and soon he was sitting on the man's lap being fed morsels.

Jimbo had a big smile on his face. "I love little dogs. I've had a few of them. They don't cost near as much to feed as the big ones, and they are good watchdogs."

"Mickey is," Lauren said. "One time last year someone was trying to break into my house at four in the morning, and Mickey barked and barked and woke me up. When I turned on the porch light, the guy took off but Mickey kept growling for a while."

"That's what I mean," the man said. "But yeah, we're bummed about Sylvia being murdered. When it happened with Billy, that was one thing, but when it happened again so soon after, in just the same way, it was spooky. But what are we going to do, ask the law to hold our hands? Most of us won't go to the shelter. If you've ever been incarcerated, the shelter is too much like a jail or a mental hospital. I been in both, and I'll take my chances out here in nature."

That made sense to Lauren. "Sounds like you're between a rock and a hard place," she said.

"Story of my life right there, ma'am."

Lauren had thought she would get Ace's advice about who to give the sleeping bags to, but he still wasn't here and besides, she just realized, he probably liked to play with the minds of these people too. She would simply figure it out. She would save one for Lee, and since Lee said he hung out with Garrett, she'd save one for him too. The others she would just give away.

She said, "I got a few sleeping bags on sale the other day, and I brought them out here for you folks."

"That's kind of you," Jimbo said. "Real kind. We've had a few snowflakes already."

"Come on up to my car and help me get them," she suggested.

A thin woman with silver strands in her wispy brown hair introduced herself as Vanessa and asked if she could carry Mickey. Lauren said sure, and Mickey let himself be picked up. At the car, Lauren said, "Gee, I wish I had a bag for everybody. How about if I give each of you one, plus I give you one to pass on to somebody you know needs it?"

"That's good," Vanessa said. "I sure hate to let go of your little dog. He's so cuddly and warm." Lauren noticed how thin the woman's jacket was, hardly more than a windbreaker.

"After you put the sleeping bags away, you can hold him some more," Lauren said. "Hey, not to be nosy, but do you folks have anyplace to keep your stuff?"

"When I was homeless in Denver, I pushed around a grocery cart," Jimbo said. "Here in the camp, we've got a plan. You can see the tents and tarps we have scattered around. Those are our homes. We take turns staying around, keeping watch. Some folks don't have time to take a turn because they have jobs in town, like at fast food places."

"I like how you cooperate, " Lauren said. "Who owns the land?"

"We, the people of the United States," Jimbo said. "What I'm saying is that it's Forest Service land. Sometimes they make us move on, but the Forest Service folks around here understand..."

"That's nice to hear," Lauren said. "My boyfriend works for the Forest Service."

"Oh, yeah, I saw you dancing with Justin at Billy's party. He's a good guy, and that brother of his, Don, is amazing at keeping cars going. Anyway, the Forest Service has all these rules about how long you can stick around before you have to move a few miles. But this bridge makes such a good shelter that there are always some people living around here, and they can't really keep track of who's been here how long. If they do tell us to move on, there are other camping spots outside of Silvermine in other directions."

Lauren reached into her car and pulled out a tarp for each sleeping bag. "I got these too, since the sleeping bags aren't waterproof."

"Great things, tarps," Vanessa said. "Those are good with sleeping bags. They cut the wind and the moisture."

"Sounds like you sleep out in bad weather," Lauren said.

"I have a nice little tent and that helps," Vanessa said. "Last year I got pneumonia and I went to the shelter till I was over it. But I like it better out here. We're like a family. And you know, I don't worry much about the killer. What will be, will be, and I think it was just Billy's time and Sylvia's time."

Lauren heard her name called. Ace was jogging down the road towards them, an hour late.

14: HIKE

JIMBO TOOK ONE look at Ace and spat on the ground. "Hey, Ace," he said, not looking at him.

"Hey yourself, Jimbo. I see you met my friend Lauren."

Clearly, they were not friends. Well, Ace could be obnoxious, Lauren had seen that. He was greeting Vanessa and fussing over Mickey, whom he hadn't seen before. Mickey was especially wary of tall men, but maybe because he felt safe in Vanessa's arms, he was licking Ace's hand.

"I have two sleeping bags left, with a tarp each, and I want to give them to Lee and Garrett," Lauren said.

Ace reacted with a look she hadn't seen. Was that a moment of gratitude? How out of character it would be. He said, "People never think of doing something nice for Garrett. How come you did?"

"I wanted to give one to Lee for sure, and he told me that he and Garrett hang out together, so it just seemed logical," she said.

He reverted to his normal inscrutable look. "They usually camp in a meadow up the creek trail. It's not a good trail, and parts are steep."

"No problem. I've been hiking all my life," Lauren countered, thinking she wouldn't put it past Ace to take her on the worst possible trail to test her. "I want to get to work by around noon, but I called the other librarian, Grace—you know, the woman who's married to a Silvermine policeman, Paul—and told her I might run late."

"That's you, always keeping your act together," Ace said. "Okay, let's go."

"Can I come along?" Vanessa asked. "Your little dog is so cuddly, I'd like to keep on carrying him."

"Sure," Lauren said. "But he needs to get some exercise. Here's his retractable leash, so he can run around a lot but not get lost running after a squirrel or something. If the trail is steep, I'm sure you'll warm up fast anyway."

Lauren automatically made a mental note of where the creek trail went uphill from the gravel road. It was just at a spot in the road where the bridge came into sight overhead if you were coming from town, and there was a long stretch on the uphill side of the road where several vehicles could park. An old red truck that looked like a permanent fixture was pulled into the bushes.

They walked up a muddy trail beside a creek. The creek was gurgling, not far from the top of its banks. Other than being slick, even the steep parts of the trail were pretty easy walking. They went up and up, until they came to a spacious meadow by the creek. They had gone high enough that there were peek-a-boo views through the trees, looking out over Silvermine. Lauren thought that when it was dark, there would be a lovely view of the lights of the town.

Lee and Garrett were dragging long tree branches over to their campsite, piling them up for firewood. Lee stopped and shook Lauren's hand. "Mighty nice to see you up here, ma'am. Do you have a message from Barb or anything?"

"Not really, Lee. She and I email sometimes, though. Is there anything you'd like me to tell her?"

"Oh, just thank her again and tell her I'm doing okay. That was such a class act, that party for Billy." Lee's eyes fell on the sleeping bags and tarps that she and Ace were carrying.

"You're not moving out here with us?" he asked Lauren. A smile played over his face, so she would know he was joking.

"No, though that would be kind of fun in the right season," she said. "My family camped out every summer when I was a kid. I learned fast what poison ivy looks like, and I got good at keeping a campfire going. These sleeping bags and tarps were on sale the other day, so I got a few. These sets are for you and Garrett, if you can use them."

Garrett had come closer. He took the set from his brother's arms and gave Ace a hug. Lauren noticed that it was a genuine hug, not just the symbolic touch that often passed for hugs between guys. He was almost smiling. "Thank you, ma'am," he said to her. "We can use things like this."

Lee said, "Ma'am, I knew you were a kind person, right from when you helped me email Barb after Billy passed." He sniffed noisily. "Something I wonder about, what makes some people nice like you and other people just looking after their own precious asses?"

"I wonder about that, too," Lauren said. "Got any ideas?"

Lee said, "Yes, I think some people have more advanced souls. Maybe people like us out here who have a lot of rough times need hard knocks to learn anything."

"I don't know about that," Lauren said. "I wish I could stay and talk philosophy with you, Lee, but I have to get back to town and go to work."

Vanessa had been cuddling Mickey close to her, and she put him down reluctantly. He ran over to Garrett, who squatted down and petted him. Lauren was surprised, as she had been when Mickey easily accepted Ace down by the road. "You must be a family of dog whisperers," she said to the brothers.

"Yes'm," Garrett said. "We get along better with critters." He was dead solemn as he said it. Why was he calling her ma'am? She was only a few years older than him, she guessed. But then she realized that Lee and Jimbo had called her ma'am too. It made her feel weird. It seemed undemocratic somehow.

Ace said, "Animals are honest. Most people aren't."

"True enough," Lauren said. "Ready to go, Ace? If you want to stay up here, I can get back to my car fine."

"I'll go down with you," he said. He picked up Mickey, who snuggled into his jacket.

Vanessa said, "I think I'll stay up here and visit with these guys a while."

Lee said, in his old-fashioned way, "We'd be most delighted to have you visit with us, Vanessa."

Impulsively, Lauren took off her jacket and handed it to Vanessa. "Here, I'd like you to have this. It's one I don't wear much and if I keep it, it will just be in my closet most of the time."

"I can't…" began Vanessa.

"Yes, you can," Lee said. "If someone wants to do you a kindness, you should accept. It's the polite thing to do."

Lauren heard him in a muffled way, while she was pulling her heavy sweatshirt over her head. It said University of Denver on it, and it was a bit tattered, with a few stains. "I never wear this anymore," she said, handing it to Vanessa.

"But you'll get cold, with just a t-shirt," Vanessa said.

"I'll run the heat when I get in my car," Lauren replied.

Vanessa said, "I've heard the expression that somebody would give you the shirt off their back, but I've never had it happen to me. You are a saint!"

"Believe me, I am definitely not a saint," Lauren said. "Just ask my boyfriend. But it doesn't take any imagination to see that you need these things more than I do. I think I'll keep these old jeans, though!"

Vanessa gave her a heartfelt hug, and Lauren could feel her ribs. Vanessa was even thinner than she looked.

15: TALKING

AS LAUREN AND Ace started down the trail, he said, "There will probably be legends for centuries about Saint Lauren of the Homeless. Don't you like the ring of that?"

"Give me a break. It's just not that big of a deal," Lauren said, shivering a little.

"Most people wouldn't ever think of doing what you did. But then, most people have less brainpower than you do, or I do, or even ol' Justin does. But it's worse than that. They are obsessed with what their fingernails or boobs look like or what kind of macho car they can roar around in. It's all about sex and money and prestige. The ones who get big time into churches can be the worst because they are so sanctimonious and often in denial about their sexuality."

"Wow, that's quite a speech," Lauren said, mentally agreeing with parts. She would never say it, though.

Ace wasn't done. "So here we are, in a world falling apart because of the idiocy. Climate change is impacting the homeless idiots — poor things, they are outside more in all weathers and many of them are so messed up that their coping skills are minimal — far more than people who can get out of the weather. I bet you've read that the homeless live thirty years less on average than housed people."

"Yes, I saw that figure but found it hard to believe. But Ace, why are you saying 'they' about homeless people when you are one?"

Ace snorted. "I don't think of myself as homeless. Well, yeah, I fit the description if you look at me from the outside, but I don't feel homeless. It's a choice I've made and I could unmake it in a heartbeat, just like I could move from Colorado to some other state. The true homeless are victims of society, and I'm not."

He went on talking as they walked, and Lauren realized he probably didn't have many people he could really talk with. He said, "All of this is a spiritual matter. I don't have any use for churches where people get together to feel good and to support each other staying in denial about what Jesus really said. But now and then, churches act on the words of wisdom that can be picked out of all the stuff in the Bible. Like the simple things of loving your neighbor as yourself or doing unto the least."

Lauren said, "I grew up rarely going to church, but my mom was big on loving our neighbors… she was always quoting that to us, and often she was doing something for a neighbor. In our family, that meant I took care of my younger brothers and sister a lot while Mom was helping a neighbor. I didn't always appreciate it."

"I had to take care of Garrett and the others practically nonstop when we were kids," Ace said. "I resented it then but it turned out to be a good thing."

"Ah, you just used the word *good*. I didn't think you would do that!" Lauren almost slipped on a tricky place in the path, glad they were almost to her car.

"Oh, sometimes. I like to mix everything up. But I do like the freedom to be myself beyond ideas of what is *good* and *bad*."

Ace's voice took on an indignant tone as he said, "Did you know that questioning authority and being a nonconformist are now labeled as a mental illness in the DSM-IV, that massive book that's used for diagnosis? This means that children like I was can be medicated into a vegetable state. No kidding, look it up. They call it oppositional defiant disorder or ODD. Pisses me off!"

"I can't believe that label," Lauren said. "I read about it in a review of the new edition and got annoyed too."

As Lauren drove home, with the heat cranked up in her car and Mickey dozing in the back seat, she thought what a complex character

Ace was. Clearly, he had a blind spot about how it could feel good to do worthwhile activities. She and Justin were both motivated by helping others, but Ace seemed to lack the inner magnet that naturally pulled her and Justin. She didn't want to believe anyone lacked it entirely, and seeing how caring Ace was toward his brother today was a hint that not everything in his head was skewed. But she still thought he could have been the killer.

16: MOMO

THE NEXT EVENING, Lauren and Mickey walked across the street and down one house to Momo's, for dinner. Mickey sniffed around the kitchen floor and found some morsels to nibble on, and Lauren suspected Momo had dropped them there on purpose. He curled up in a corner of the kitchen for the evening, snoring a little every now and then. One time, his little paws got busy as he dreamt something exciting.

"This is great timing for me to come see you," Lauren told the older woman. "After going out to the homeless camp, my mind has been swirling around, and I've felt off balance. I haven't even told Justin that I went there… haven't been ready to deal with anyone else's emotions about it."

Momo laughed. "We made this date last week, so I guess I can't claim I was psychic about the timing. Or can I? The nature of time isn't only linear… But tell me about your visit. Come get some squash soup first, and the salad is on the table."

Momo and her husband had bought the house when they were raising their daughter, Betty's mother. After her husband died and her daughter went away to college, Momo rented out two of the three bedrooms to college students for a few years, stretching the income she had from life insurance. Then she turned the dining room into her art studio and gradually began earning her living from her unique paintings. Betty had lived with Momo for a while before she married Don, and she had planted shrubs and trees around the yard.

As they ate in Momo's cozy kitchen, Lauren told Momo about the second death of a homeless person and about her trip to the camp. It was wonderful to have someone in her life she could say everything to. Momo was the least judgmental person she knew. Being a boomer and growing up in the sixties had left her alternative-minded but open to normality too. It occurred to Lauren that most people couldn't handle alternatives and Ace couldn't handle normality.

"I'm reflecting on the symbolism of the rocks that have been put at the feet of the people," Momo said. "You said they are Crestone Conglomerate?"

"That's what I heard," Lauren said.

"My friends in Crestone call them 'Baca Rocks,' and they are lovely. Have you seen any?"

"No, I just heard about them being left at the feet."

"They're found in all sizes from smaller than your thumb to huge boulders," Momo said. "They come from the mountains called 'Sangre de Cristo,' or blood of Christ, that go all the way down into New Mexico. I wonder if there is any kind of meaning or symbolism in referring to the blood of Christ. It makes me think of compassion. I don't know if the rocks are found anywhere outside the Crestone area, though. I have several in my back yard that Ace gave me recently. I'll have to ask him about the meanings. Oh, he did tell me once that 'Sangre de Cristo' refers to the reddish tones the mountains often take on around sunset."

Lauren registered only one part of what Momo had said. "You know Ace?"

"Yes, since he was a child. He's very intuitive, maybe he told you that. He started having past-life visions in his teens."

"I didn't know any of that."

"No reason you should have."

"Does Justin know that you've known Ace for years?"

"I doubt it, not unless Ace told him. When they were all teenagers, Betty and Don hadn't gotten together yet, and I didn't know the Russells well till after she had her psychic awakening in high school. I know she told you that story last year. Well, Betty probably met Ace briefly here back then, when she lived with me for a while."

Lauren leaned forward, over the table. "Did you know Garrett too?"

"Not well. Ace brought him by here once or twice. I remember how opposite he and Ace were. Ace was always talking and thinking, and Garrett seemed shut down, like he had a weaker life force, you could say. I got the feeling it was past life stuff weighing Garrett down, but I never did a reading or anything. Ace worried about him, and we talked about it sometimes back then."

Lauren said, "I think either of them could be who Billy called a bad man. One guy at the dance hall thought either one of them could have murdered Billy. What do you think?"

Momo said, "I walked into the conversation in the dance hall kitchen that night and I turned right around and left the room. I often stay away from emotion-laden conversations where I don't want to get a blast of what people are thinking but not saying."

Lauren asked, "You didn't want to know if Ace was involved?"

"No, actually, I didn't feel the need, but more than that, I could feel a lot of blame and sorrow and confusion in the kitchen. But I can say this, Ace is more amoral than most people, and it's hard for people to understand where he's coming from. I wouldn't do quite a few of the things he does, but generally I don't judge others for their choices. You know the old saying about not judging unless you walk a mile in their moccasins… I'd just as soon stay in my own shoes."

Momo went into her studio and came back with a photograph she handed to Lauren. "I did a portrait of Ace a few years ago. The original is in a gallery downtown, but the photo captures the feeling."

The portrait showed Ace's head, shoulders, and chest. He was looking right at you out of the picture, with his characteristic challenging look. He was wearing a tie-dye t-shirt, but the colors around him and the shirt were more intense than the shirt and much busier in design. Momo pointed to a section of the the colors and said, "That's where the energy is centered. He's a complex blending of light and dark, clear and murky."

"I've noticed that," Lauren said. "This is interesting. I wonder what a portrait of Justin would look like. You haven't done one, have you?"

"No, I haven't," Momo said. "I'm seeing that it would likely be in greens and browns, as he is so tied into nature. Also, I often use lighter browns—tans, actually—when someone is methodical or a researcher, and he's both. I'd have to capture his quirky little smile, maybe looking sideways out of the canvas. That would be fun to do. How are things with him?"

Lauren admitted he was annoyed with her for letting Ace sleep in the library, and then she remembered she wasn't going to tell anyone else what she had done. "Please don't share that I did it," she said. "I'm in trouble with the library board about it."

"Actually, I knew. Margaret and I have been close friends since fifth grade, and she couldn't keep it from me. She was over here one afternoon for a cup of tea, and it happened to be the day she had called that meeting. I took one look at her aura and had to clean it. I couldn't help but pick up what had happened. She also asked me to keep it secret and of course I will. I'm good at secrets. Once, years ago, I was in a polyamory threesome, and nobody knew."

"What's polyamory?" Lauren asked.

"My word, girl! You don't know what that is? I was in a love relationship with two other people, a woman and her husband. We were dedicated to being clear and honest with each other about everything. I didn't live with them, but we spent a lot of nights together, and we did everything you can imagine."

Lauren said she was sure she couldn't imagine.

Momo chuckled. "That was several years after my husband died, just after Betty's mother had gone away to college. When the couple moved away due to work, I never wanted so intense a relationship again. I was already selling some paintings then, and I just wanted regular lovers after that, since my painting needed everything I could give it."

"Holy cow," Lauren said. "I had no idea. So is that why you never married again?"

"I love my freedom," Momo said. "Once my art began selling steadily in galleries, I made enough money, but I needed to be able to paint whenever I wanted to, sometimes late at night. I also need a lot of time in meditation in the inner worlds, and not every man would understand—or like it if he thought I should be cooking dinner for him. So I've just found that boyfriends are best for me. Take Arnold. Have you met him?"

"No, I haven't, but Don has spoken fondly of him."

"Yes, he and Arnold are good friends. Well, Arnold's wife died a couple of years ago, and he learned about the next world because of that. They and I had been friends for years, and recently Arnold and I progressed to lovers. You wouldn't think a free spirit like me would fall for a state patrolman, even though he's retired, but Arnold is so caring. Really, I'd call him devout too."

Lauren said, "He sounds great… I remember hearing that he goes to the same church as the Russells. Say, I've got a bit of a problem I wonder if you could advise me on. An old girlfriend of Justin's in Fort Collins seems to be after him. Don and Betty went to see him last weekend, and Don said the woman was crawling all over him."

"Let me take a look," Momo said. She dropped her gaze downward, toward the crocheted tablecloth, for a moment. "There is no real love between them, just a line of bright red energy between their pelvises."

Lauren felt her face get hot. "What about between our pelvises?"

Momo said, "With you two it's not just that, it's everywhere, like you are in a golden bubble together, lots of light and love. It's a more general life force, but it's got plenty of sexual energy too."

"As I told you, he's still annoyed because I let Ace sleep in the library. It's not like I let Ace into our house."

"Oh, but symbolically it's the same," Momo said. "I always think about symbolism. What I'm picking up is that Justin has feelings of jealousy towards Ace, and he's acting out a bit."

"He thinks I'm obsessed with the homeless," Lauren complained.

"Well, yes, you are. But it will pass. Your aura shows a sense of rootlessness, which seems to be from your childhood. It's a big part of why you have taken Silvermine so much to heart."

"Would that show if you did a painting of me and my aura?"

"Your aura is bright. I will paint your portrait if you want to come sit for it. It's in the sitting that the real soul of a person jumps out at me, so I can't say off the cuff exactly what a painting of you would look like. I can work from photos, but I wouldn't with you, since you live so close."

Lauren said, "Sure, I would love that, whenever we both have time. Do you ever do couples together, like Justin and me?"

"Marry the boy and I will do you two in one portrait," Momo said, "But that's not reason enough to marry him!"

"Yeah, I just don't know if that's ever going to happen," Lauren said. "Say, could I do some photo portraits of you sometime? I love photography."

"That would be fun," Momo said. Lauren went home feeling way better.

17: BOARD

GRACE SAID, "RING, ring, Silvermine Public Library, can you hold while I empty the bucket? Thank you." She and Lauren were playing with ideas for a skit they would do at the upcoming library board meeting.

Grace set down a pretend phone and took an imaginary bucket halfway across the staff room, mimed tossing the water out the door, and came back to set the bucket in its spot before picking up the pretend phone.

"Thank you for waiting, I was afraid it was going to spill over onto the whole floor. How can I help you? You want to renew some books? I'm sorry, our computers are down after last night's rain shorted them out. Just bring the books in when you get a chance. We've increased fines to ten dollars a day to raise money for a new roof, so please take your time about bringing the books back."

Lauren laughed. "Great start! Let's see. I'm a patron… Can you help me find a dry book in the mystery section? They seem to be all wet over there."

"Yes, the sweet little cozy mysteries are sopping, but the thrillers with sizzling sex have been drying out from all the heat, so they are merely damp. Please take a bunch home with you and put them near your heater," Grace said.

"But what if I set my house on fire from them being close to the heater?"

"Then your insurance should pay our fees for the replacement costs of the books."

They both laughed. "This has possibilities," Lauren said.

They developed it more later. Ashley, working at the circulation desk, gave them some ideas based on the many ways people tried to avoid paying fines. The autistic shelver, Daniel, suggested gestures in a couple of places. He was always quiet, and even this time, he didn't say much. He just showed what he meant by doing it.

Lauren was apprehensive about the board meeting. Her embarrassment about the night she let Ace stay in the library hadn't diminished, and she hoped the little performance would ease any awkwardness. She and Grace ended their skit in a position Daniel had suggested, down on their knees begging for pennies for the roof, while holding pretend umbrellas over their heads. The whole board applauded enthusiastically.

"This is way too funny to be forgotten," Margaret said. "Make it longer, use props, and you could do it at fundraisers."

"Or I'll video it for YouTube," another board member offered. "Maybe it will go viral."

"Excuse me, but I'm going back to the reference desk," Grace said. "I didn't know I'd signed up for an acting career when Lauren hired me."

Lauren passed around pages to the board members. "This shows the best three bids for a new roof, with how soon they can do the job. The stapled pages are a list of people and organizations in Silvermine to meet with regarding fundraising for a new building. The third item is a proposal for a day-long library board retreat I'd like to facilitate on a Saturday in January."

"I'd like to volunteer to have the retreat at my house," Virginia Wagner said. She was the newest board member, having taken on her husband's position after he died in the stacks the previous year. "I'll take care of the food too. If you have any allergies, tell me beforehand."

Everyone would attend after her offer. Virginia's charming country-style house and gourmet food were well known. The food was not to be missed.

"Lauren, there is one more item I'd like to add to today's agenda," Margaret said. "Could you give us an update on how our outreach to the homeless is coming along? I'd also be curious to hear how they are affecting other library patrons when they are in the building."

Lauren noticed immediately that Margaret said "our outreach." That sounded like code to her, that the board was generally with her in terms of the homeless. Or at least, Margaret was.

"Gladly," she said, writing it in at the bottom of her agenda. "I'll go through my ideas for the retreat now. I want to begin with a visioning process, looking at what a new library could do better than we can do now, or what a new library could do that we can't even do at all here. I read an article written about the Pikes Peak library system, around Colorado Springs. It said libraries were changing from being like supermarkets, where people took what they wanted off the shelves, to being like kitchens, where the library could be a place where people cooked up collaborative creative projects." She promised to provide a link to the article, and a couple of other good ones, before the retreat.

She went on, "We can have a mid-morning break with some of Virginia's famous cold-process coffee."

"What's that?" a new board member asked.

Virginia answered. "I'll show you how I make it at the retreat. Basically, I roast and grind my own organic coffee beans, though you could start by buying beans that were already roasted and ground. Then I soak the ground beans overnight in a carafe filled with cold water and in the morning I decant the liquid. Because the beans never touch hot water, the coffee has a much smoother taste. It only takes a couple of tablespoons per cup, and that's if you like it strong."

Lauren said, "I didn't realize it was that easy, Virginia. I'll have to make a habit of doing it at home and bringing it in to the staff room. So back to planning our retreat… with caffeinated brains we can brainstorm what the library building might look like. We'll need citizen input so we won't come near making any decision at the retreat, but we can talk about it. I would guess that most of you have seen how the library in Salida added a wing onto their old Carnegie building. If you haven't, try to to drive there and look around sometime before the retreat."

She asked Virginia to make the lunch light, to keep the afternoon session lively. They would come up with goals and plans, and people would sign up to do things. Someone suggested t-shirts from one of the online places like Cafepress or Zazzle.

Margaret turned to Lauren and asked for her report on the homeless in the library.

Lauren's palms became sweaty as she spoke. She told the board that there were several homeless people who were using the library. Mostly they did a little email or read for a while, and sometimes they dozed off in the armchairs. "Some of them do have strong body odor, and several of our regular patrons have complained to me or Grace about that. We just tell them it's a public library and that means it's open to the public, but several have complained loudly and repeatedly. I rearranged a couple of the comfortable chairs to be quite a ways away from the others, and the homeless people are naturally gravitating to those." Lauren had seen the homeless carefully analyze where they could sit, away from anyone who looked normal.

"Grace has been planning with people at the shelter," Lauren added. "After the holidays, she is going to start doing a story hour there after school once a week, and we are going to put one of our free book boxes there in the shelter, with both children's books and ones for adults."

Margaret took Lauren out to lunch after the meeting. They waltzed around the topic of what secrets Momo knew, and by the end of the meal, they understood each other perfectly. They both knew there was no keeping secrets from Momo.

18: BROTHERS

LAUREN WOKE ON a Friday morning feeling great. Why? Justin would be home for the weekend, but being with him was still a combination of stress and pleasure. Her thirtieth birthday was the next day, but she hadn't been thinking of that. It must have been the great dream she had just been having. A group of smart, creative people had been working together in delight.

What were they doing? Lauren stayed in the same position in the bed that she had been in as she woke up, and she closed her eyes and tried to go back into the dream. The feeling of creative collaboration was very strong, and she saw several people gathered around a work table. That was all she could remember.

She bounced through her morning exercises and walk with Mickey. She decided to go in early to work even though she didn't really need to. The dream had her feeling so buoyant that it would be a good time to make more notes for the January board retreat. If it went half as well as her dream, it would be fabulous.

Richard was cleaning the library as usual, and she told him her dream. He said, "I'm glad to see you chilling out. You've been pretty intense lately, with all the homeless issues. I wondered if you would burn out."

"Well, I feel like I'm getting back on track with working toward a better library. Maybe that's what my dream was about. Hey, how is Sunshine?"

"She is going to be in a Christmas crafts fair in Denver. It was a hard one to get into, as it was juried, and they liked both her cross stitch and her needlepoint. I don't expect to see much of her till it's over… She will be sewing night and day, but she is happier than I have seen her in years. Partly that's because she's excited about making a decent amount of money. She's got a small disability income, but earning from her crafts is a whole new game for her. I think she's made about fifty bucks on etsy and that gave her confidence a boost, but this show is huge."

Lauren pointed to the wall, where a cross stitch that Sunshine had done was hanging. "It's great having her 'All you need is love' here. It has sustained me quite often. But I am guessing that there might be another reason she's happier…"

She remembered uncomfortably that Justin had warned her that being curious could be construed as being nosy. But she really wanted to know if Barb's frank talk with Sunshine the weekend of Billy's party had helped. She forgot for the moment that she was Richard's boss, which made it even dicier to ask personal questions. She was just thinking of him and Sunshine as her friends.

Richard laughed. He kept mopping as he said, "Yeah, she's better… A couple of times she's had flashbacks, and I've been able to help her let go of them. We're taking it slow, though."

He mopped vigorously. Lauren turned to her computer.

*****

Friday afternoon, Lauren was organizing a few things downstairs in the staff workroom. There wasn't much she needed to do before the weekend. She heard loud thumps coming down the stairs… it sounded like Ace's boots.

It was. He came into the workroom and flopped down on the sofa.
"What's up? You look discombobulated," she said.
"Nobody's come in and told you?" he asked.
Her heart skipped a beat. "Told me what?"
"My brother almost bought the farm," he said.

"No, I didn't hear a thing. Tell me."

Ace looked distraught, his eyes moving this way and that as he spoke. Lauren had never seen him like this; he had always been cool and mental. "It happened this morning, at first light. Lee and some other guys saved his life. Lee woke up when he heard Garrett babbling. The first thing he saw was one of those rocks at Garrett's feet. Then he saw a syringe on the ground. Garrett was sitting up, leaning against a tree, real disoriented."

"But he survived?"

"Yeah, he was lucky. He and Lee happened to be sleeping at the bridge last night, and Lee knew that Garrett's best chance for survival was if he got a drug called naloxone. Lee hollered for someone with a car to take Garrett in to the ER, but one of the guys at the camp said he had a dose of naloxone and knew how to use it. He had picked it up from people he knew in Denver the other day, after Sylvia died, just in case there was another attempt. So he gave it to Garrett, and he and another guy are taking care of him. They seem to know what they are doing."

Lauren could imagine how she would feel if this had happened to one of her brothers. "So someone went and got you?"

"No, I was sleeping in my van, quite a ways away, near Crestone. I woke up this morning with a worried feeling. I couldn't tell what it was, but my sense was to get to the camp as fast as I could, so I did, and they told me what happened. I've been hanging around Garrett most of the day, and he's going to make it. I came into town to get some groceries and stuff."

Lauren wondered why someone would try to kill Garrett, but this didn't seem like the time to ply Ace with questions. "Thanks for letting me know," she said. "I'll say some prayers for him, if you don't mind."

"Couldn't hurt, could help."

"Also, Justin is here this weekend. Come by my house if we can help you out in any way. You know where it is, right near Momo's."

"Okay, appreciate it."

Ace went back up the stairs and left. Lauren just sat for a bit and said, "Garrett" as a prayer.

Then she said, "Ace."

She went on, "Garrett… Ace… Garrett…Ace…"

19: THIRTY

EVEN THOUGH THEY had no new ideas about where they could live, Lauren and Justin tried to pick up their relationship as if the rift was fixable. He got back to Silvermine around dinnertime on Friday, and she had a beef and veggie stew cooking in her crockpot. They had a pleasant enough evening, nothing special, but the stiffness between them was melting.

As Lauren woke up in the morning, Justin whispered "Happy birthday!" in her ear. They weren't in any hurry to get up, and there was a lot of love in their cuddles. Eventually, Justin cooked up a big omelet —from eggs they got from Betty's hens—and he put thirty little candles on it. Lauren started to blow them out, but he said, "Wait, did you take enough time with your wish? It's going to come true, you know!"

She had wished to marry him and for them to live happily ever after in Silvermine, both of them contented with their work. It was a three-part wish but it kind of fit with being thirty, and she wanted all of it. She blew the candles out in one breath.

Over breakfast, Justin asked, "So how do you feel about turning thirty?"

"It feels fine," Lauren said. "I feel mature in a good way, more able to tackle the world. I can even see that if it isn't a new library building, it will be something else. But don't tell Margaret Snow I said that about the building! I just mean that I feel more able to contribute my energies as they are needed, and that life will show me what to do."

"Wisdom becomes you," he said, and leaned over the table to give her a kiss.

"By the way, I had a conversation with Ace that I haven't had a chance to mention to you," Lauren said.

"Haven't had a chance or haven't wanted to hear what I would say?" Justin grumbled, but it was a teasing grumble.

"It just happened yesterday. Remember I told you that there had been a second death out at the camp, a woman who died the same way Billy did?"

"You mentioned it on the phone."

"Well, Ace came in the library yesterday to tell me that someone tried to make Garrett the third victim, using the same method. Ace looked really shaken. When we talked, it seemed like Garrett was going to pull through." She went over the details that Ace had given her.

Justin said, "Sounds hard on Ace, since he's been such a big brother to Garrett all his life."

"Yeah, it obviously was hard for him. I've never seen him like that. I haven't been able to figure out who would have done the killings, or even whether they were done by the same person. Nobody seems to care much," she said.

"That could be," he said.

She said, "Oh, by the way, yesterday I told Ace that you were home for the weekend and to come by if he needed any help."

Justin's eyebrows shot up. "How does he know where we live?"

"Didn't I tell you that he is a friend of Momo's?"

"Nope, I didn't know that. It kind of figures, as they are both such out-there characters. Well, I can't imagine what help he'd want from me. I don't expect we'll see him."

"Probably not," Lauren agreed.

They planned to walk in the park with Mickey and around six they would go over to Betty and Don's for a family dinner celebrating Lauren's birthday. Betty had insisted that Lauren didn't have to cook anything since it was a feast in her honor, and Betty had included

Justin in the ban. It was fun to have a whole day to do whatever they wanted to.

20: QUESTION

AFTER DASHING AROUND the park with Mickey in a drizzle in the late afternoon, Lauren and Justin were home making coffee when someone knocked. "Maybe that's Ace," Lauren said.

It was. Justin invited Ace in for a cup of coffee.

"I don't have much time, but thanks."

Ace took a roundabout way of explaining why he had come by. "Justin, from your Forest Service work, do you know the meadow where people sometimes camp, up a ways from the bridge?"

"Yes," Justin said. "When I was working in the Silvermine district, sometimes I had to go out there and check on things."

Ace turned to Lauren and said, "You know the place I mean, the highest we climbed up to."

She nodded, wondering if she had gotten around to mentioning that outing to Justin. From his frown, she knew she hadn't.

Ace noticed the frown too. He said to Justin, "Lauren and I just went to the first camping area on the trail, that little meadow, taking stuff to Lee and Garrett, but you've gone further up?" Lauren thought he could be diplomatic when he wanted something. She doubted he would have come to see them unless he had some sort of request.

"Yes," Justin said. "There are a couple of big old cattle ponds, one higher than the other, both of them above that creek trail. But if they spilled over, I don't think all the water would go into the creek bed. If I remember correctly, it would spread out in a couple of other directions too."

Ace said, "I haven't been out there since early this morning. After I got up, I parked my van in one of the other places I use, not at the camp, and walked into town. I've been talking with Momo just now. I was about to jog out to the camp and check on Garrett. It worries me to think of them camping in that spot tonight."

He explained further, "Jimbo hiked up above the meadow earlier today. He saw a trickle of water running downstream from the lower cattle pond, along a little gully that is usually dry. It made him wonder if the pond were to wash out, if it could flood the meadow and the creek trail. He knew I was going into town so he drove in and found me at my usual coffee shop. He told me that he didn't notice Lee or Garrett around, but their gear was in its regular place so he figured they were going to camp there tonight."

Justin said, "Right below where the pond could wash out… You know, it's been a few years since I was up there. It could be that either of those ponds might flood where they camp."

Ace said, "I can check on things by myself, but Lauren had offered your help, and even if I jog all the way, it would be totally dark before I could get there. Also, I thought that with your Forest Service experience you might be more able to read the signs of what the water is doing—or even have more ideas on how to get the guys out of there, if there were any problems. They are usually wasted by this time of day, which won't help with hiking out."

"What do you have in mind?" Justin asked.

"If you and I take your truck out there right away, we can get up to the meadow where they camp by right around dark… before dark, I hope. Each of us could help one of them down, partly supporting them if we need to. I don't think I could do both guys in one trip. The camping area down by the bridge wouldn't flood, so they could sleep there. I don't know why they even went back up the trail this morning. Jimbo said Garrett was insisting he was fine…"

"So, Ace, are you picturing us coming straight back down the creek trail with the guys?" Justin asked.

"Depends on what we find. It's the shortest way and it's the way they are used to. But if it seems dangerous near the creek, we can go the other way. From their camping spot, with your back to the creek, if you walk straight across the meadow till you get to a line of trees, under the tallest tree there are some old truck tracks. Must have been how ranchers drove close to the old cattle ponds. It's easy walking back down to the road that way and it's away from the creek," Ace said.

He continued, "Justin, I don't think we would be in much danger going up, because we could watch out for signs of flooding and climb the side of the old creek bed in time." Ace thought a moment and added, "Probably, but no guarantees. Maybe I shouldn't have come."

Justin said, "I can take care of myself out there. Let's get going fast, Ace. Lauren, I'll take the truck and then you can go over to Betty and Don's in your car and meet me there. I'll come straight there for dinner."

"No," Lauren said.

"No?"

"I'm coming with you. We could all be needed. Remember, I hike and climb fast. I will call Don and Betty while you drive. Ace can hop in the back of the truck, there's some soft stuff under the camper shell to sit or lie on, and even though it's been raining so much, I happened to check this morning and saw that the back is dry."

She thought out loud, "Let's park right at that spot on the gravel road where the old red truck is parked. I'll tell Don the truck will be there. Let's grab a few first aid supplies, some drinking water, energy bars…" She was collecting things from around the kitchen as she spoke. She tossed most of the contents of her purse into her daypack, grabbed her walking stick, and put on her hiking boots and coat.

"Sure, you're right, all three of us is better," Justin said. He gathered his stuff and gave each of them a large flashlight with good batteries in it. As they all left in the truck, Mickey barked his displeasure at being left behind.

As Justin drove, Lauren phoned Don and Betty but had to leave a message. "Hey, it's Lauren. Justin and I are driving out to the homeless camp with Ace. He thinks a meadow might flood and he asked us—well, he asked Justin but I'm going too—to help get his brother and Lee out of danger. We might be a little late for dinner. If we aren't there by seven or so, maybe Don and Pete could come out and see if we need any help. We'll be parking Justin's pickup near an old red truck that's in the bushes on the gravel road, and right after that a trail goes up beside a creek… we'll be going up that trail. I'll keep my cellphone handy, but I doubt there is service along the creek as it's in a depression and phone service is iffy out there anyway. See you soon, bye!"

"That shouldn't be necessary," Justin said. "But Don likes to know what's happening so he will appreciate it."

Lauren said, "Agreed, it shouldn't be, but I like to have just-in-case plans."

"Yeah, I know, you're like Don." Justin lowered his voice so Ace couldn't hear him from the back of the truck. "Hey, were you as surprised as I was when Ace asked me for help? He has never, ever, asked me to do anything for him."

"I think the conversation I had with him yesterday, about Garrett almost dying, showed me a vulnerable side of him, and that's why I invited him to come by if we could help. He's bound to know you have outdoor skills that could be useful."

"I hope we don't need them," Justin said. "Here we are, but I'm going to turn the truck around so it's facing town. And Lauren…"

"Yes?"

"If the guys have gotten real muddy or wet by the time we get them down, would it be okay to let them clean up in our bathroom?"

"Never thought I'd hear you say that," she said. "Sure."

21: UPHILL

BY THE TIME they started up the trail, it was dark under the trees. Clouds were thick overhead, and a few drops of water dripped down their necks or onto their rain hats, but it wasn't raining. Ace led, as if there was no doubt that he would. Justin gestured to Lauren to go next, and she figured that he wanted to keep a protective eye on her and maybe to keep her going fast.

The trail was just wide enough for one person. Ace was moving right along without using a flashlight, and Lauren thought that he probably had good night vision from the way he lived. Justin hadn't turned his light on, either. Was that a guy thing or did he also have great night vision?

Well, she would turn her light on. The trail was slippery in spots, and every little indentation was a puddle. The creek was musical beside them, right up to the top of its banks, fuller than it had been when she came with Ace the other morning, but then things looked different in the near-dark. She watched a rock, larger than she could pick up, moving erratically downhill in the water. There was a mysterious beauty to the night. It was chilly, and a breeze made it colder, but Lauren was warm enough from hiking up the trail rapidly.

Nobody spoke. All three of them were concentrating on the trail, avoiding mud puddles and rocks. Lauren was almost able to keep up with the pace that Ace was setting. Every now and then he would turn impatiently and pause until she and Justin were up with him.

As they climbed, the trees thinned out and the sky showed a little light to the west. Lauren watched Ace's silhouette, with gray clouds behind him, as he moved fast. She thought he seemed like a woodland creature himself, at home in the wilds in a way that few Americans were any more. Yet even a century ago, many people would have been. It felt to her like a loss.

Justin's mind had been on more immediate topics. He turned on his flashlight and pointed its beam onto the hillside to their left, where they could see the ridge on the same side of the creek as their trail. "If you hear a roar of any sort, even a faint one, scramble up there as fast as you can," he said, ostensibly to Lauren but loud enough that Ace couldn't miss hearing. "Don't wait to figure out if it's an airplane overhead. No telling how much time we would have for a margin of error."

"That would be if the pond had broken?" she asked.

"Yes, if it were to give way, it could happen slowly at first and then suddenly whoosh," Justin said. "But if that guy who hiked up to it earlier did observe accurately, the slow part may have been going on for hours already. This is actually more dangerous than I expected, since the wall of the old creek bed is so steep along here."

"We're over halfway to the camping spot," Ace said. "The walls get easier to climb in a little bit."

They continued uphill in silence. The trail was right next to the creek here, and it took more concentration to stay out of the muddy spots. Again, she enjoyed the beauty of the night. What better people to be out with than these two? Each in his own way had a lot of experience outdoors. She'd done a fair amount of night hiking herself, come to think of it.

Justin asked, "Ace, how wasted are these guys likely to be? Do you think there might be more than just the two?" Lauren knew from the questions that Justin had been considering possible scenarios they could have to deal with. She appreciated how thoroughly he thought things through.

"I think it will just be them. Jimbo said the other guys who sometimes camp up there have settled into a tent near the bridge. As for wasted, Lee is just a drinker, not a druggie, but he could have a good bit of wine in him. And he's been getting frail lately. Justin, if you take him, I think you'd have to support him but not carry all his weight."

Ace went on, "My brother uses whatever he can get, booze or drugs. I may have to support him at first, till he gets the idea that we are going down the trail. He's used to doing what I tell him to, so once he gets it, he should be able to walk out. … Lauren, maybe you can grab any gear of theirs that you can carry down."

"Okay," she said. "Hey, what if they aren't there?"

Ace said, "Then let's go down the old truck track. It's possible that they know about it and might be camped along it, if they have any inkling of danger from the waters."

Ace could talk and still hike quickly. Lauren admired how deftly he moved along the wet trail.

"Might the wetness of the trail through here be related to that pond leaking?" she asked.

Justin spoke immediately, and Lauren thought to herself that there was a subtle competition going on between the guys. They both loved being the expert.

He said, "I doubt it. If the pond is leaking, and I am not convinced yet that it is, its waters might not come this far down. I think they would spread out at that camping spot."

Ace said, "Yes, right, Justin. I've been along this trail several times lately and it's been this wet or even wetter. You've probably both noticed the raw earth between the creek and the trail in several spots, where the bank has given way."

"We haven't had this much rain any year in my lifetime," Justin said. "It's rearranging the landscape all over this part of Colorado."

Lauren figured he was about to make a comment about climate change, but suddenly she heard him exclaim, "What the—!"

She turned to see him sliding down into the creek as the trail gave way. He was upright, at least. She thought he was about to get very cold feet and legs, but she didn't sense any danger.

But evidently Ace did. He turned, brushed past Lauren, and grabbed her walking stick as he went by. He ran downstream and called out, "Justin, grab this!"

Water was up almost to Justin's waist in the creek. He was keeping his balance by waving his arms and by moving with the water, but he was just too far downstream to reach the walking stick. As he disappeared out of sight, Lauren heard him yell something.

Ace tossed Lauren's walking stick back towards her, hollered "Justin!" at the top of his lungs, and dashed downhill along the trail.

She could hear them both hollering to each other, but she couldn't see either of them. She grabbed her walking stick and followed after them down the trail.

Their sounds became fainter. Then she couldn't hear a thing except the creek. Feeling more anxious, she hurried faster down the trail. Her flashlight revealed a gap in the trail, where part of it had collapsed since they came up. She slipped part way into the gap, going down into thick mud on her left side.

Slowly, she pulled herself up. Things had changed so fast, but what had happened? It couldn't be serious, could it? A short video she had seen on Facebook came unbidden into her mind. It was only three or four minutes long, but in that time a large creek, or maybe it was a small river, took out both lanes of an ordinary paved two-lane road. She doubted there would be that much force in this water, but she thought uneasily of how just a few minutes ago she had watched a heavy rock move downhill in the creek. She hoped Justin had climbed out of the water.

22: ALONE

LAUREN'S INTENTION WAS to keep moving downhill after the guys, but she couldn't see how to get around the mudslide she had just fallen into… it was a little too wide for her to jump over. Shining her light down, she saw that the area in front of her was filling with creek water, making a pool. Shining the light away from the creek, she saw open land where the slide had stopped—but within a couple of feet it became dense shrubbery. She was pretty sure that if she tried to go around the edge on the bit of open land, she would just slide down again.

So now she couldn't go downhill right along the stream. She'd have to take a different route. At least, she wasn't too cold. A coating of mud went along her left side, from her boot, up her jeans and part of her coat. Her elbow hurt, but not badly. She could see her walking stick, stuck in the mud near the top of the slide. It must have helped break her fall. She extricated it from the mud, glad to have it. She didn't often walk with it, but now it was like a companion.

But what had happened to her two human companions? How far downstream were they now? The sound of the creek, so charming earlier, kept her from hearing anything else. She called both names several times, but heard nothing but the creek.

She had been holding panic at bay, but now she couldn't quite manage it. She was shaking.

She wasn't thinking clearly. Maybe they were in trouble. Maybe Justin had lost his balance and gotten wet from head to toe. Maybe he was drowning right now, in the cold, fast-moving water. Maybe Ace was trying to help him or maybe… Lauren couldn't believe where her mind was going. She had been picturing Ace holding Justin's head under the water, howling in a primal triumph as his longtime rival drowned. Where did that come from?

But someone was a serial killer, and it could be Ace.

"Chill," she said to herself, and felt a glimmer of humor at her choice of wording.

She told herself to breathe. She took several deep breaths, and they gradually became more even. Stamping her feet to keep warm, she could feel the fear receding. It was right on the edge of her consciousness and it would come back if she let it.

"Time to make a list," she thought. "One, follow them cautiously down the trail. No, I just saw I can't do that. Two, try my cellphone and call Don if it works. If it doesn't work, panic again…no, not a plan. Three, continue on the rescue mission uphill and if Lee and Garrett are there, get them over to the old truck track. Four, stay here but I don't know why I'd want to. Maybe Justin and Ace are fine but way down hill, and maybe I'm in more danger than they are. Five, observe my surroundings. The creek is running higher now, and the trail has more water on it."

The list was a start. Doggone if she didn't feel calmer. The panic felt like it had moved further away from her. She felt a bit of advice, not in words but if it had been words it would have said, "Don't put your attention on the fear, as doing that will bring it back in. Notice the calm and let it envelop you."

With all the things to do on her list, she felt like she was wasting time, but still the advice made sense. "Peace," she said out loud, thinking that now she sounded like a hippie from the sixties. "Peace."

Suddenly she felt calmer. She didn't feel alone any more. She felt the presence of a friend, a loving and humorous friend. It was more like Momo than anyone else she knew, but even Momo was just a shadow of this.

"Good God," she said in disbelief.

Then she laughed out loud. God must be exactly who this friend was. But she would save theological speculations for later. She just stood there, cold, her elbow hurting, confused about what to do… and none of it really mattered. How weird was that? She basked in the feeling of support engulfing her.

That helped her to think more clearly. "First, do no harm," she said out loud, and then she wondered what the Hippocratic oath was doing in her mind at this moment. Oh, it was telling her not to risk harming herself. That meant that whatever way she moved, or even if she stayed put, she should care for herself as the precious gem that she was. Precious gem? That was an odd thought too.

She looked at what she could see in the range of her flashlight. She couldn't easily go either upstream or downstream along the trail. Okay, check, remove them from the list. That made sense if the creek might be rising.

Lauren didn't think her cellphone would get a signal there. But before she could reach for the phone to try it, she felt a compelling inclination to get away from the creek. Okay, Justin had suggested climbing up to the ridge, and Ace had mentioned the old truck track. She would climb up and see if she could find the old track. In any case, up on the ridge she'd have a straighter shot out toward the lights of Silvermine and better cellphone reception.

Suddenly, she was clambering along a deer trail going diagonally uphill. She saw fresh-looking droppings on the trail and felt relieved. If it was a current trail, maybe it would take her where she wanted to go.

With her flashlight in one hand and her walking stick in the other, she followed the trail. She wondered what had happened to her sense of time, as it seemed like only a couple of minutes until she was on the crest, looking out over the lights of Silvermine. How pretty they were.

23: HELP

LAUREN PULLED HER cellphone out of the side flap of her pack, expecting that it was going to work since she was on higher ground. She was surprised when she looked at the time on it. Only quarter after six now. That was just after the time she and Justin were due for dinner at Don and Betty's. Her birthday dinner. Well, it was hard to imagine but maybe they would be celebrating together soon, all of them. They could even invite Ace.

Don answered her call on the first ring. "We're glad to hear from you," he said. "Betty had a powerful vision of fast-moving muddy water in a creek over its banks, and it gave her a very worried feeling."

"She's right," Lauren said. "I'm okay, but Justin fell in the creek when the bank gave way. I lost sight of him after he went around a bend in the creek. Ace went down the trail after him, but when I tried to follow, I couldn't go that way so I had to climb up to get to where my cellphone works. Can you come out here and help find them?"

"We'll be there pretty quick. Dad is on his way over here now… we were going to go anyway, after Betty saw that water. I know the area, I've worked on cars out there. We'll park near that old red truck."

"Wear boots and watch out for a possible creek rising from a pond above that might give way," Lauren said. She said she was pretty sure she could meet them near the old red truck. But she told Don that if she wasn't there, they shouldn't wait for her before looking for Justin.

"I'm cold and muddy," she said, noticing her body in an abstract sort of way. "If I see from your vehicle that you've arrived, I might go on home in Justin's truck and take a hot shower before going over to your place for dinner. But if Justin's truck is still there, that would mean I haven't found my way down the hill yet. Ace said there is an old truck track that goes on down to the gravel road from where I am now. I have a good flashlight and I'm going to try to find that track. It should be easier walking. Oh, and cellphones only work in some places out here."

"I've been up that truck track, a couple years ago. Hey, Happy Birthday!" Don said.

"I hope it will be," she said. "I'm guessing that Ace would have gone further up the trail looking for his brother, but you could holler some for him. I did that already, without any luck."

Trying to get her bearings, Lauren circled the beam of her flashlight around the area, looking for the old track. No luck. She took several deep breaths, and her calmness increased.

She worked her way downhill, keeping the lights of the town visible. They kept her company, just as her walking stick did. Odd how these things could feel like companions, but she'd take friends any way they came just now.

Half slipping and sliding down a muddy stretch, Lauren saw ruts from pickup trucks. Relieved that she must be on the old track, she walked more rapidly. Maybe she would get to the gravel road before Don and Pete. She thought of what good people the Russells all were, in a crisis or any time. She was lucky to have hooked up with them. She started to get scared again when she thought what Justin might be going through. That boulder she'd seen earlier bumping its way downhill was a clue to the force of the water. At the very least, he would be plenty cold.

She wondered what he would have done if he had gotten out of the creek easily, right after he had disappeared. Well, she didn't have to wonder. She knew. He would have gone looking for her and he would have found her soon most likely. So that didn't bode well… She hoped she'd know soon enough. She could imagine Don and Pete going uphill to look for Justin, Justin working his way uphill to look for her, and then what? Hmm, maybe she was the lost one.

She assumed Ace would head up the hill to look for his brother. Well, for Lee too, but she didn't think Ace was really searching for anyone but Garrett. Maybe they weren't even camping up there. But wherever they were, she knew better than to try to go find them alone and risk getting herself into a worse position. She thought of the last time she had seen them, how courtly Lee had been, and how even Garrett had managed a rare smile. That had been a good morning.

What if the pond was going to give way? The thought made her feel cold again. She wished she knew if her worries were groundless. She shook with another chill. At least it was easy walking down the track. Like everywhere in the forest this autumn, the ground was soft from all the rains. You couldn't drive up it now.

She hurried along. It felt good to move faster... until she tripped on a small shrub and went sprawling.

That was stupid, she scolded herself while lying on the ground. Gingerly she began to get up. Her left elbow had gotten whacked again, and it hurt more this time. As she began to stand up, her left ankle hurt. It wasn't a sharp pain, but it was still plenty sore. Grateful for her walking stick, for the first time all evening she really leaned on it.

Slowly she continued down the track. She couldn't see any lights from the town now. She was too low for that, but she did hear the sound of a couple of trucks. What a relief to see their headlights. So both Don and Pete had come out in their trucks, unless it was someone else. She lost sight of the headlights, but she could hear doors slamming shut and men calling to each other. A woman's voice said something she couldn't make out. It sounded like Justin's mom, Sue. They could have her birthday dinner right here, Lauren thought. Then she realized that wasn't a rational idea. Geez, she must be out of it to be thinking like that.

Another few minutes took her onto the gravel road, and a moment later she was in Sue's arms.

    Lauren began to cry hard, her shoulders shaking, as Sue held her.

24: SEARCH

SUE HELD LAUREN in a tight embrace until her shaking subsided. Then she held Lauren out at arms' length, looked at her mud-splattered clothing, and said, "Here, let me have your coat and you can take this heavy blanket."

Lauren just stood there. Sue tugged on her, as she would with a child, and got Lauren's coat off. She tossed it into the bed of Pete's pickup. Lauren moved her ams to help remove it, but she didn't seem to have any inclination to do anything more.

The warmth of the blanket felt good. Sue opened the passenger door of the pickup and said "Hop in." Lauren obeyed, and Sue tossed Lauren's pack in, at her feet.

Sue started the truck to run the heater. It was considerably newer than Justin's, and since they had just come out in it, there was a heavenly blast of heat right away. "Lauren, Pete and Don are out looking for Justin and Ace. We should know something pretty quick."

Lauren nodded. She had been feeling like she wasn't in her body. "They call this stress," she said to herself, as she wriggled to let the hot air flow over different parts of her body.

"Thanks, Sue," she said. It was good to be with her. Justin's parents had been incredibly helpful last year when Lauren had stayed with them at their ranch on the edge of town. That was when it was too dangerous to stay at her own house. She felt so safe with Sue and Pete. They were both practical, take-charge people.

It dawned on Lauren that this had to be hard on Sue. Lauren and Justin had been a couple for less than two years, but Sue had carried Justin in her womb, held him as her firstborn, and—with Pete—raised him and Don to be strong and self-reliant men. Lauren knew, from helping to raise her siblings, that showing so much confidence in children wasn't easy on parents. You had to let the kids make a lot of mistakes. She said, "It's got to be hard for you too, not knowing what's going on out there."

"Sure, it is, but I can't count the number of scrapes the boys have gotten themselves out of. Justin may be thirty, but it feels right now like he's a kid again. Both he and Don gave me gray hairs early, I swear. Pete's pulled a few scary things, too!"

Sue was quiet for a moment and then went on, "My faith gets me through times like this. You know, it's not a simple thing, that I pray and then get what I want. It's more that I somehow know there is a bigger picture that includes whatever happens, whether I think it's good or bad."

"Yeah, sometimes I get there," Lauren said. "After I got separated from the guys up the hill, I felt like I had a loving friend with me."

"Tell me more about that when you get a chance," Sue said. "Now, let's plan a little. Pete and Don will be back here sooner or later, and maybe Justin and Ace too. If everyone is okay, you all can have hot showers and we'll have a late dinner. But do you need to go to the emergency room, Lauren? You were leaning a lot on your walking stick."

Lauren slowly felt her ankle and her elbow. "I don't think so, Sue. I can tell better later, but I'm okay for now."

"Well, just keep monitoring your body. If Justin or Ace needs first aid, the guys can do it. If either one needs more, we'll take him to the emergency room or we'll call an ambulance."

Lauren appreciated how Sue was thinking through the options. Maybe Justin got that from her. Sue hadn't mentioned two other possibilities: that they wouldn't be able to locate Justin, or the worst one of all. She wondered if Sue knew that yet another possibility was that the creek could flood any time.

"What was Betty's vision?" Lauren asked.

"Don said that she felt sick when a vivid picture came into her awareness and stayed there. She saw muddy, fast-moving water in a creek at the top of its banks."

"That's what it was like," Lauren said.

Sue said, "She also felt anxiety along with the picture. That's not usual for her. I got the feeling it might have reminded her of that time when she was in high school…"

Sue stopped abruptly. They both knew what she was referring to, but now wasn't the time to think back on it.

They talked a little about dogs and about cross-stitch, both of them with their ears strained for the sound of the men coming back. Sue opened the driver's window a few inches, so they could hear better. Lauren updated Sue about her visit to the homeless camps, how they had tents made of tarps and so on. The time seemed interminable.

Finally, they heard footsteps. Don came up to cab of the truck, his face grave. "We found Justin, and he needs an ambulance… he's got a broken leg at least," he said. "You two drive till you get a cell signal, then call 911 for an ambulance out here as fast as they can send it. I think all the dispatchers know where it is if you say the homeless camp under the bridge, but be sure the person you talk to does know. The drivers should know anyway, but just be sure so they can get to Justin soon. Tell them to watch for me, here near the old red truck, and I'll take them to Justin. Then go get Lauren cleaned up and meet us at the hospital."

Lauren had hardly breathed while Don was saying this. "Anything else the matter with Justin?" she asked.

Don looked at her, his blue eyes kind. "We found him unconscious, and he's been going in and out of seeming to know us since he heard our voices. He's lying close to the creek, and his right leg has got to be broken from the position it's in. We didn't check for further injuries on Justin. We'll leave that to the paramedic.

"We didn't see Ace. We hollered repeatedly and didn't hear anything back. I'm going to grab blankets and stuff from my truck and get back there. Then I'll leave Dad there again and come down to the road to watch for the ambulance. Oh, tell the dispatcher that both Dad and I can help carry the stretcher, we've had experience. Lauren, give me the keys to Justin's truck and I'll bring it into town. Love you both!" He kissed his mother's cheek through the truck window, took the keys from Lauren, and was gone.

"Could be worse," Sue said. "Seatbelts, please." She took off like a shot down the road and got the truck moving fast.

Lauren pulled out her cellphone and kept checking it. "I've got a signal," she said to Sue.

Sue pulled over to the side of the road and asked for the phone. Lauren passed it to her. Sue called 911, identified herself, and told them everything Don had suggested to say. She did it in an efficient and friendly manner, and she added a couple of things to Don's message: that Justin was her son and that he had been out there on a rescue mission himself.

"They'll get right on it," she said to Lauren as she handed the phone back and started speeding again.

Lauren was shaking again. Sue said, "Now let's go to your house and you take a long hot shower while I call Betty. We'll have time to do that and still get to the hospital in good time. You need to take good care of yourself now, Lauren, because Justin is going to need you big time."

"I didn't think of that," Lauren said.

"I did. He's going to need lots of help from all of us, and he's going to get it," Sue said. "Of course, we'll help you too, anything you need."

25: HOSPITAL

DON WAS WATCHING for Sue and Lauren when they arrived at the emergency room. After quick hugs, he said, "The crew got out there real fast. Since Justin was a ways from the road, they took the stretcher. The paramedic was a woman I know, and she's topnotch. She gave Justin enough of an exam to be sure that he could be moved after they stabilized his leg. He wasn't talking but he was grunting when things hurt, and I could tell he was communicating with us with those grunts."

Don went on, "Dad and I followed the ambulance here, and they let Dad stay in the room with Justin most of the time while I did the paperwork. Dad came out just a few minutes ago and said that it looks like a broken leg and a possible concussion. Justin is pretty much out of it. He's going into surgery for the leg pretty soon."

Justin could recover. Would recover. But what about Ace? She asked and Don shrugged his shoulders.

"I want to see Justin," she said.

Don said, "See that blue curtain that is pulled all the way across down there? See where I'm pointing, Lauren?"

"Yes."

"That's where he is."

Lauren walked down the hall and into the cubicle. Justin looked terrible, his head showing a bump on one side, and his leg held in place by something. Pete was sitting in a chair holding Justin's hand. He smiled at Lauren.

"Hi, honey," she said to Justin.

He tried to open his eyes but squinted at the bright hospital lights and kept his eyes shut. "Hi," he whispered. "Okay?"

"Yes, I am, and you will be. I love you so much, and I'll see you soon," she said. She grabbed his hand, gave it a squeeze, and walked out in tears.

"Your turn," she said to Sue. Lauren sat with Don and said to him, "Justin looks terrible."

"He looks great to me now," Don said. "Imagine seeing him worse than that and out there by the creek."

"Good thing I didn't see that." Hot tears ran down her cheeks. She leaned over, put her hands over her face, and sobbed.

"Oh, Lauren, it's hard, isn't it?" Sue said as she came back. "Here's the latest. They are just about to take him to the operating room, and he will be out of it after that. He doesn't need any of us now, so I suggest we go over to Don and Betty's and eat dinner. We didn't expect your birthday dinner to be like this, but we have a lot to be thankful for."

"Okay, let's go have my dinner," Lauren said. She would be glad to get away from the hospital.

*****

Before they ate, they held hands and Sue led them in a prayer for Justin. Lauren felt like he was there with them. Over dinner, everyone caught each other up on what had happened. Lauren told a short version of the story of the friend who had been with her when she was alone, but enough for Betty to nod vigorously.

The others sang happy birthday to Lauren, and she felt it was one of her best birthdays ever, because of the way it was turning out.

Sue said, "We want to have someone with Justin as much as we can at first. Lauren, you desperately need a good sleep, and Don and Pete, you both worked hard out there, so I should take tonight's shift. I don't know if they will let me be with him after the surgery but there is something hard to resist about a determined mother." She grinned. It was good to see her smile.

"Tomorrow morning, how about if Pete comes in to spell me around six? And we can figure out a schedule for the day. With any luck, tomorrow Justin will be able to tell us what happened."

"If someone is going to church tomorrow, I might like to go along," Lauren said through her exhaustion.

"I will," Betty said. "I'll pick you up just before ten."

Lauren slept the sleep of the dead and didn't wake till late. She was relieved that she wasn't limping. Her elbow hurt a little, but it was nothing she'd need care for. She had just enough time to walk Mickey briefly and have a bite before Betty came by, with Rosie making little talking sounds in her car seat.

They went to the Episcopal church. Sue had phoned the church the night before, and Justin had been put on the list of people needing prayer. When his name was said, Lauren felt a huge wave of love going to him. It didn't feel like it had to do with any distance. It just felt like power. She thought of how Sue had gunned the motor of the pickup truck. It was sort of like that.

Betty dropped Lauren off at the hospital before going on home with Rosie. "Keep me posted," she said. "Sometimes people assume that because I'm psychic, I know everything, but I don't."

Lauren promised, and then she walked in the front door of the hospital, which was much quieter than the ER entrance had been. Still, the hospital vibe was there. She asked for Justin's room number at the front desk, hoping they wouldn't say she couldn't go there. But the woman working just said, "203," and pointed down the hall to the elevators.

When she walked into Justin's room, she saw Justin, with Pete sitting by him. There was another bed in the room, but nobody was in it. Pete smiled at her and said he'd go home. Justin was lying down in the bed, with an IV tube. His broken leg was elevated, but she couldn't really see what it looked like because of a blanket covering him. He opened his eyes as she came in.

"Hi, babe," he said. He sounded so ordinary.

"You sound wonderful," she said.

"Hard to talk."

"What happened?"

"Later?"

"You want to talk later, Justin?"

"Yeah, resting." At least he spoke more than he could the day before.

He dozed for over an hour, Lauren sitting in the room with him. She looked out the window at the hospital parking lot, with its rows of small trees, while all sorts of thoughts went through her mind. Was his mind affected? Legs could heal, and she had the passing thought that they weren't essential to personality, but what if he had lost part of how his mind worked? She knew concussions often healed but how long would it be before they would know? She felt her body tightening. In her head, she could hear Momo's advice to breathe deeply but she couldn't do it.

Don came in, and that woke Justin up.

"Hey, Don," he said.

"Hey, Justin, what happened?"

"Umm… fell in the creek, it was deep… a boulder banged me into another one… Ace dragged me out."

He winced. "My head hurts."

"You probably have a concussion," Don said. "You should feel better later, and you should be able to talk better too. But we can understand you… you are making sense."

"Good," Justin said.

"Mighty good," Lauren said. "And you have a broken leg too."

Justin tried to move his legs. The left one moved fine but the right one barely changed position. He grimaced.

Don said, "Dad and I found you lying by the creek. You were in and out of consciousness while we got an ambulance and brought you here to the hospital. You had surgery last night. But you don't remember any of that?"

"Nope. Glad I wasn't there." A flash of a smile crossed his face. Lauren and Don grinned at each other. That comment was pure Justin.

26: BROKEN

A DOCTOR CAME into the room and told Lauren and Don that Justin's broken leg was something called a femoral shaft fracture. He showed them an X-ray which indicated that Justin's femur—the large bone between knee and hip—had been broken, just above his knee. Justin's surgeon had inserted a metal rod and special titanium nails in the femur. These items would provide a strong and stable positioning and would also remain in place permanently. No cast was needed. Justin's break had not been an open fracture, with its greater risk of infection. He had some big bruises, though.

Justin would use crutches to get around at first, and follow-up visits would be required to assess when he could switch to a cane and then to nothing. A full recovery would take months, but Justin's athleticism and youth would help him. Justin would be able to speed things up by being diligent with his physical therapy.

The doctor said the concussion seemed to be a mild one and would likely clear up within days or weeks. When they told him about Justin's little joke, he said, "That's a good sign." He added that Justin had no sign of the problems he could have had if he had breathed in or swallowed the muddy creek water. Lauren was glad that was one issue she hadn't even thought of.

He couldn't give them the exact date that Justin could leave the hospital, but he said, "He'll be able to go home quite soon, and you folks should arrange to have someone with him all the time at first. You'll need to set things up to help him with everything around the house." One form of help would be making sure Justin took the antibiotics, pain meds, anticoagulants, and any other meds he was given, on the right schedule. Another would be driving him to appointments.

"Piece of cake," Don said. After the doctor left, he told Lauren that he had talked with his parents about their work schedules. It would be possible—if not quite a piece of cake—to have someone with Justin whenever Lauren had to work.

"I have a good bit of personal leave I can take, too," Lauren said.

"Good, I'm sure we'll all manage fine together. So now, I'm here, and you're off duty till tomorrow morning."

Lauren went home and collapsed on the sofa with Mickey. She lay there wondering what Ace had done after he pulled Justin out of the creek. Why hadn't he helped him beyond that? Maybe he thought she would turn up there any minute, but he wouldn't have expected her to be able to get Justin down the hill. Maybe he just was so obsessed with helping his brother that he couldn't do anything else. Sure, he had done the first step in saving Justin's life by pulling him out of the creek, but if others hadn't come along, it still could have been curtains for Justin.

It was all so close still that Lauren shuddered. She was going in and out of a scary feeling of vulnerability. Well, it wasn't going to be curtains for him. He was under good care at the hospital, and his powerful, determined family—including herself—was ready to do whatever he needed.

She still felt angry at Ace for abandoning Justin there. She wouldn't have done that, and she thought it was dirty of Ace to have left. "I'm really mad," she said out loud to herself. Mickey had been dozing on the sofa next to her. He raised his head, licked her a few times, and went back to sleep.

But then she suddenly realized that Ace could have been injured too. Why hadn't that even crossed her mind until this minute? Her anger dissolved completely. She hadn't been thinking clearly with the stress. What if he had been lying out there himself all this time? What if…? She stopped her over-active imagination by a force of will.

Was there anything she could do now to help Ace if he needed it? She knew that Don had notified Search and Rescue, and he would have told them everything he knew, which was pretty much everything she knew. She sent a wave of loving energy out to Ace and to the searchers and let go of trying to do more now.

She tried to think through what could have happened. She guessed that most likely Ace hadn't been seriously injured and that he had gone up along the trail again, not impeded by her slower speed. He likely made his way up to the meadow where Lee and Garrett camped. But the creek had been pretty full as she, Justin, and Ace went up, more than they expected. If it could throw Justin around, it could cause even more harm to guys who were so wasted. No wonder Ace ran off to check on them, assuming he did.

If he'd found them, Ace would have taken Lee and Garrett over to the old track and walked them down that way… it would have been some time after she was gone from the track. Getting the guys down would have taken Ace a while. She wondered where he had parked his van the day before. He was pretty cagey about sharing personal information, and all he had told them yesterday was that he had moved the van to another place and walked into town. The van could be anywhere around Silvermine.

She'd better do some practical things with the rest of her Sunday. She remembered that she had the number of Justin's boss in Fort Collins, from a time when Justin had used her cellphone to call the guy. She dialed the number and a man answered.

"Hi, this is Justin Russell's girlfriend…" Lauren suddenly realized her words could sound alarming, so she went on right away. "He broke his leg yesterday, near Silvermine, and I wanted to let you know."

Justin's boss wanted to know exactly what had happened. Lauren mentioned the concussion but downplayed it. She promised Justin would be in touch as soon as he could be. She was moved by how much concern the man voiced. He said, "You must know it yourself, but Justin is one very special person. We think really highly of him here, not only because he's got that brilliant mind but also because he's such a fine human being."

Lauren's eyes teared up at his comments. She thanked him, got off the phone, and stretched out on the sofa again, where Mickey's warm little body comforted her. She dozed a while.

When she woke, she thought she'd better learn how to get the house ready for Justin's return. She sat up with her laptop and googled "broken femur." She skimmed through some medical pages that made her gag. But she also found advice written for the person with the problem. She started a list of things to do: pick up throw rugs, make sure there were no electrical cables that would be in the way, send small pets away for a few weeks…

Nope. No way was Mickey leaving. He would be company for Justin and he didn't get underfoot much. Well… maybe he did. But he and Justin could learn how to share the space. Mickey was one of the smartest dogs she knew. With his Sheltie herding background, he might herd Justin around! Lauren smiled at the thought.

She got a few more ideas online, and then she walked around the house. Hmm, was there spacee in the bedroom for a king-sized bed? Her queen had been big enough for them, but as soon as she had the idea, she went back online and got the measurements for a king. Yes, they could get one and she thought they would both sleep better with the extra space.

By bedtime, she had a list of things to do, prioritized and with notes on who could help her do them. Luckily, she was in good enough shape financially that she could buy the bed, the living room futon sofa she was imagining, and a few other things, without going into debt. She liked it that way.

27: FLOOD

NO FAMILY MEMBERS were in Justin's room when Lauren walked in on Monday morning.

"I sent them home last night, because I didn't need them here overnight," Justin said.

"That was a good sentence, honey. How's your mind working?"

"Better, I think," he said. "I don't remember much, though. What happened?"

Lauren told him what she and Don had told him the day before, and filled in more details about it all, including the ambulance trip. Then she asked, "Do you remember anything about Ace?"

Justin wrinkled up his face as he thought. "Sort of, but I'm not sure… I think my leg got smashed between a rock moving in the water and a huge stationary one, and I hit my head on the big one, and then he pulled me out of the creek."

"Yeah, that must be about it… I didn't know all that exactly, but it makes sense. Ace disappeared after that."

"I could have drowned if he hadn't pulled me out. How did I get to the hospital?"

Lauren said, "I told you that part a few minutes ago. Can you remember it?"

"You did? No, I don't remember."

"They say you have a concussion, so that might be why you don't remember. I think it's already getting better, though, because you are talking better today."

"Good," Justin said. "I'd miss my mind if I didn't have it."

Lauren's cellphone rang. It was Sue, touching base. Lauren told her

Justin seemed quite clear mentally. Sue said, "Well, I've got some news. It isn't good, but I didn't want someone else to blurt it out so I guess I will just blurt it out myself!" She told Lauren.

"That was your mom, and she had some bad news," Lauren said. "Shall I tell you now?"

"Of course."

"One of the search and rescue people called your folks to tell them that the creek and meadows did flood late Saturday. Yesterday, they found the bodies of Lee and Garrett. They drowned in a pool that formed at their campsite when the pond up above gave way."

"The fate I escaped," Justin whispered. He was quiet for a spell and then he asked, "But how about Ace?"

"He hasn't been found, but those Western boots he always wears were stuck in the mud, near Garrett's body. The search and rescue people looked all over that area for him after they found the boots. Jimbo was with them and he identified the boots as definitely belonging to Ace."

Lauren began crying as she spoke. Justin reached out his arms to her. She stood close to his hospital bed, avoiding his IV tubes, and they hugged and cried together.

*****

After she got home, Lauren phoned Barb in Wyoming. She began," We've had quite a lot happen here this week, and some of it is sad."

"Honey, don't keep me in suspense."

Lauren told her about Lee's death first thing, as she knew that would mean the most to Barb. Then she went through all the other events.

"Never would have expected all that, but there is a beauty in it," Barb said.

"Beauty? I sure didn't think of it that way..."

"Well, you know, Lee didn't have much left to live for. He was missing Billy something fierce. He and I talked on the phone some after you helped me get that cellphone to him, and all I heard from him was sadness and discouragement. So now he's in the next world, with Billy, and their sufferings are past. As for Garrett, well, Ace told me some, and he was another lost soul. I like thinking of them all in Heaven."

Lauren asked, "But what about Ace? Do you think he's gone too?"

"Honey, I sure don't know. I don't mean that he'd have gone to the other place... I'm not sure there is any place but Heaven. If you ask me, I think we all go to a place of such enormous love and light that people who did really bad things can't bear the light till they grow up some more. As for Ace, I don't know if he is going to turn up again. He's very resourceful and... well, you know, he can be devious. Have you thought that he might have disappeared for his own reasons?"

"No, I didn't think that," Lauren said. "It could be. I've been mad at him for leaving Justin alone by the creek but now I'm worried about him."

"Oh yeah, that's tough. You handled it really well, doing what you did. Well, this story isn't over yet. So what's being done about the bodies of Lee and Garrett?"

"They will be cremated at the mortuary you used."

"If you want to pick up those ashes, next time I come down to visit, we can do something with them."

Lauren was surprised. "I didn't know you'd be here again, with both Billy and Lee gone now."

Barb laughed. "You haven't seen the last of me. A big chunk of my heart is in Silvermine."

"Well, good," Lauren said. "By the way, with how things have unfolded, I don't know if we'll ever find out who killed Billy. It bothers me not to know what happened. I think I told you that a woman at the camp died in the same way Billy did, but you may not know that Garrett almost died in the same way last week."

"Darlin', I really don't care if the mystery is solved or not. I don't like to think of the homeless tied up in the legal system. They suffer so much when they lose their freedom and get treated worse than trash… I saw it with Billy a couple of times when he was in jail just for being drunk and getting in fights," Barb said.

"I didn't think of it that way," Lauren said. "You're a wise woman but I can't let go of wanting to know."

"Just keep going along and life will make you wiser, honey," Barb said. "That's how it works. You'll learn a lot from having your boyfriend stuck at home like that. If the two of you don't hate each other by the time he's healed, you'll know you've got a lifelong love that can take anything, like my hubby and I have. And I bet it'll go that way for you."

"I sure hope so," Lauren said.

28: THRILLERS

JUSTIN HAD STARTED physical therapy by the next day when Lauren went to see him at the hospital. He had been walking with crutches in the hospital corridors, and they had given him pages showing stretches to do, to keep scar tissue from hardening. Justin was going to be working a lot on his recovery, all right.

He said, "I have a favor to ask of you. It's boring here, and they say I'll still have pain for a while. Would you buy me a bunch of thrillers for my Kindle? Really gripping ones will help me forget all this." He waved a hand around the room.

She offered to check out some mysteries from the library. "Maybe sometime," he said. "But I really like reading on my Kindle in the middle of the night. And can you bring it and my charger to me today? It's on my side of our bed."

Later, she asked for recommendations from an online group of Colorado librarians she was part of. Others responded quickly with enough ideas to keep Justin reading for a long time. They sent her lots of good wishes, as she had posted that her boyfriend had broken his leg.

She took the list and logged in to Justin's Amazon account. Several of the librarians had recommended John Sandford's *Prey* series, and when Lauren saw that he had written a series with over twenty titles, she bought Justin the first three: *Rules of Prey*, *Shadow Prey*, and *Eyes of Prey*. She shuddered just reading bits of the reviews. Evidently Sandford was great at creating really horrible villains. But the reviews also said that the hard-boiled hero was fabulous. The term "ice blooded" kept turning up. Well, whatever it took to keep Justin's mind off his troubles!

Lee Child was another name the librarians mentioned repeatedly. Again, there was a series, so she bought Justin the first three: *Killing Floor*, *Die Trying*, and *Tripwire*. Scary, she said to herself as she looked over the blurbs.

She went to Amazon's bestsellers in thrillers and mysteries, looking for more of the authors the librarians had liked. She found David Baldacci's *King and Maxwell*—she wouldn't sleep if she tried to read that before bed. She added John Grisham's first novel, *A Time to Kill*, considered his best by some, but she knew she would never read it.

Exploring the depths of human depravity would never be her cup of tea. Justin would use these books to escape, and that seemed reasonable to her. If she were in his shoes, she would read obsessively too, and she would read mysteries, but not these.

She had recently discovered a genre called cozy mysteries. They generally had one or more murders, but not described in gory detail. Figuring out who committed the crimes was a puzzle more than a journey through agony. Cozies went easy on graphic sexual descriptions and on foul language, too. Often they had recipes and food featured in them, and the name of the genre was from their settings in cozy places, like cute little towns.

She would load up on Leighann Dobbs, Gemma Halliday, Cindy Blackburn, Carol Lee, Jerusha Jones, and a bunch of others. On her laptop, she had Amazon's top one hundred cozy mysteries page bookmarked, and she went there now and then to keep up with what was new. Come to think of it, she should get some more cozies soon, as they were such good distraction and she could use plenty of that now.

When she took him his Kindle later that day and told him what she had loaded on it, Justin was pleased with her selection of thrillers. He said that the nights were long in the hospital, even with meds that were supposed to knock him out and control his pain. Now he could self-medicate by reading.

"Speaking of sleeping…" Lauren said, "I'm going to buy a king-sized bed after I leave the hospital. It will make things a little crowded in the bedroom, but I think we'll sleep better. I've shopped around and I'm going to go lie on some mattresses and choose one."

Justin smirked. "I care more about who's in the bed than what kind it is. I've been whiling away the long hours by picturing how we are going to…"

"I've given that exactly one passing thought," she said.

"Nothing the matter with this boy's hormones," he said, with another smirk. He sure was cute when he smiled like that. His dark brown eyes locked on hers and she felt a thrill she didn't expect to feel while visiting a patient in the hospital.

"Did you ask the doctor how long we should wait before bouncing around?" she asked.

"Of course not," Justin said. "What if he said we should wait?"

They planned a few more details for when he got home. "I'm glad your normal personality is coming back," she said.

"But I'm still forgetting things too much."

"I can see you improving from one visit to the next, though. Say, I've been wondering whether you regret going out there when Ace asked you," Lauren said.

"Not a bit," Justin said. "It was the right thing to do."

She reached over and gave him a hug. "I thought you'd say something like that. You're a great guy."

"Aw, shucks," he said. "Just let me show you how great I can be."

"Justin! We already talked about that. Have you forgotten so fast?"

"I do remember. Now that I have something good to read, maybe I can think about something else," he said.

29: HOME

DON BROUGHT JUSTIN home from the hospital in an old minivan he had picked up for them to use while Justin couldn't easily ride in a car or pickup. Watching the two brothers get out of the van, Justin doing as much as he could on his own, Lauren felt gratitude more than any other emotion. Sure, she still wished the accident hadn't ever happened, but she thought of herself as a realist. It had happened. Now he'd be home with her. How ironic that this would begin the longest stretch of living together that they had had so far.

She had bought a long futon sofa and a recliner for the living room, and a king-sized bed that left them enough space to walk around in the bedroom, even with crutches. With Don's help she had everything in place, along with some more prosaic changes like handles on the bathroom wall and a strong railing out front. Justin approved of it all.

The minute they were alone, he suggested to Lauren that they try out the bed. He had been thinking of some inventive positions, and with the help of the new pillows they figured out a good one. "It's so good to be with you here," she said as they snuggled afterwards. "I know it's just been a few days, but so much has changed."

"Yeah, I could have died."

"And thanks to Ace and your family, you didn't." She asked Justin, "Why did he just leave you there, do you suppose?"

Justin said, "I have a memory of him pulling me up away from the creek onto the land. I mostly remember the pain in my leg as he dragged me by my armpits. Oh, now I remember… part of my mind was going 'No, don't drag someone like that till you check them for spinal injuries,' but it was an abstract thing. I don't think I was worried that I had some. I also remember the relief when he let me go and the pain level dropped, and I was totally on land instead of in the water. But his leaving me alone there, I just don't remember what happened next."

Lauren said, "This is going to sound really weird… I had an image of him drowning you."

"Yeah, that is strange all right. You've got a weird mind."

She said, "Well, I was just about to say something about how much I love you…"

He said, "Sometimes your mind works magnificently! What were you going to say?"

She looked at him lying there on the bed, the new handwoven striped bedspread pulled up around him, his right leg propped on the extra pillows. "I was going to say that I love you tremendously. When I didn't know what had happened in the creek, I realized—more than I ever have—how much I love you. When I saw you in the emergency room before they operated, I willed you to be fine, with all my strength. Of course, I expected you to, but a little extra intention or prayer never hurts."

"Aw, sweetie," he said. "Gimme another kiss."

She did, a long, lingering one, hugging him close. She went on, "I realized that I love you so much that being with you is more important to me than anything else. Justin, this is huge. I am willing to move to the Front Range with you and give up my Silvermine job, if that is what is necessary for us to stay together."

"That's wonderful," he said. "We'll just have to see how things unfold. It's going to be weeks at least till I can drive, and months till I have full mobility. So we'll have a lot of time right here in Silvermine, enough time to evaluate everything."

"Let's not mention to anyone else that I would consider leaving my job," she said. "I wanted to tell you, but let's not make it a topic of conversation with the rest of the family or anyone else, okay?"

"Sure, I understand. Let's see what you think of me after I am a grumpy convalescent."

"Oh, I know you'll be terrible at times. But I'll abandon you if you're intolerable." She smiled to be sure he knew she was joking. "You know I'm taking some time off from work, but Don, Betty, your parents, Momo, and maybe some friends will also be taking turns being with you. I'll arrange it so that whenever you get majorly grumpy, someone else comes in!"

"All this help means a lot to me. I wish Ace could come too."

Lauren asked, "Do you think he is dead?"

"No. I can't wrap my mind around that idea. I can accept Lee's and Garrett's deaths. But Ace… I don't think so."

"We should ask Momo what she sees."

"Good idea," he said. "Now, if you would be so kind as to give me a hand, I can't get dressed by myself. I want to do some of the stretching exercises the physical therapist showed me."

It took a while for them to get his clothes on him. How had they come off so much faster?

30: BETTER

"HEY, LAUREN, GOOD to see you," Richard said as Lauren went back to work after a few days off.

"Thanks, Richard, it's been rough, but Justin's in a groove now, in between physical therapy, having the whole family waiting on him, and reading thrillers. Did you hear what happened?"

"Yeah, it was in the newspaper and I've got some friends out at the camp. And Grace filled me in on what happened to Justin. If he needs another strong guy to help out sometime, you've got my cell number."

Lauren was moved by Richard's offer and thought it might be handy. She asked, "How is Sunshine?"

"I think she's doing well. She doesn't want to see me while she's obsessing on her needlepoint for the crafts fairs. We just talk a little, but that's fine. I'm taking some pretty accounting heavy courses at the university, so I'm busy too."

Lauren settled down to tackle her library emails and planning lists. Since her attention had been so caught up with Justin, she had hardly given library matters a thought. She did the emails quickly, trying to build up some momentum before getting into work that would take more emotional energy. There were quite a few messages from other librarians, wanting to know how she was doing and what thrillers Justin liked best. She wrote one email for everyone, a short one saying things were okay, Justin was home, and he was inhaling a thriller a day, usually reading till late in the night.

She called Margaret Snow with a few work details. They chatted a bit about Justin's broken leg. Margaret asked "Any word on the homeless guy?"

"You mean Ace? No. They found his boots in the mud near his brother's body. He may have gotten away okay, but nobody has seen him."

"What times we live in. At least the rain has been letting up a little."

"Yeah, making way for snow soon," Lauren said. She didn't mind Margaret asking. They were getting back on friendly terms. Besides, who knew what Momo and Margaret talked about? Lauren still adored the sense of community that existed in Silvermine, but she had seen lately how difficult it was to keep anything secret.

Later, Lauren started a list of things she knew how to do around the library that Grace didn't. She should train Grace in all of those. After all, if Lauren had been the one with the broken leg, Grace would be acting director. In the afternoon, she and Grace met in the staff room, went over the list, and then took a coffee break together.

"I had the most amazing experience when I was by myself in the mountains after Justin and Ace disappeared," Lauren confided. "I felt like I had a good friend with me, wise and even humorous… my stress level went way down."

"I'm glad the Lord was with you," Grace said.

Lauren said, "It was great, but I didn't feel that it was male or female. Tell me, Grace, if you don't mind, why do you call it the Lord?"

"It's Biblical, and I grew up using that language. If you speak of Spirit or God or the Virgin of Guadalupe or any other name, I have no problem knowing what you mean. The Lord has many faces and encompasses both genders. I just give thanks that you had that gift of the Presence."

"I do too," Lauren said. "I wanted to tell you this part, which I don't talk about with most people."

"Thanks, I'll be quiet about your personal experience."

They went back to work refreshed. Lauren thought how much nicer it was to work with Grace as the other librarian than it had been for her first year here, when she worked with the much lazier Deanna Ward. She wondered for a moment where Deanna was now, but the thought didn't linger.

*****

Lauren had told Richard that Justin was getting into a groove, and he really did seem to be. Justin was even more methodical than she was, and he put a calendar up in the living room, listing which family members were coming when Lauren would be working. He listed the stretches and exercises he had to do each day, and checked them off. He had his physical therapy and medical appointments logged, along with who was driving him. He loved being able to take part in the family potlucks, and he was beginning to get rides over to Don and Betty's or to his parents' place, just to visit and hang out. He had progressed to not needing caregivers with him every moment.

Mickey had been puzzled at first by Justin's crutches and awkwardness but he soon adjusted. He frequently curled up next to Justin on the new futon sofa.

In between his scheduled events, Justin often napped, annoyed that he had to, but he still had pain and didn't sleep well at night. He read thrillers whenever he could, and Lauren often woke up in the night to see him stretched out on his back reading his Kindle.

Justin didn't pick up after himself yet, and could be quite lordly about telling people what he wanted. And as he had threatened, at times Justin was grumpy. "Do you have to make so much racket?" he asked Lauren one evening as she was running the vacuum while dinner cooked.

"No, I could let the house get filthy instead," she said.

"The noise hurts my head," Justin complained.

"If you go into the kitchen now, you won't hear it so much, and I can get the whole house done before we eat." Lauren had learned fast not to baby him, even though she often wanted to.

"I think you would benefit from a good massage. My friend Kathy is great," Lauren said to him over dinner.

"Never had one," he said. "Why start now? All this is costing a pretty penny, and my insurance pays for the physical therapy."

"Yes, but a full massage could help your whole body reintegrate. Want me to call Kathy and make an appointment? Hey, I'll make it a present and pay for it myself."

"Thanks," he said. "That's nice of you. But I'd be embarrassed if I had an erection while a woman was touching me. Other than you, of course!"

Kathy was an avid hiker and skier, in excellent condition, and nice looking. "Never thought of that," Lauren admitted. "I'll ask her if it happens much."

She sent her friend a Facebook message and got a reply, "Yes, it happens sometimes. I just ignore it and continue on."

Justin reluctantly let Lauren make an appointment, Don drove him over, and he came home a convert, with another appointment soon. "Your turn to pay, though!" Lauren said.

"Hey, I don't mind. I think I've been missing out on something worthwhile!" He moved around more smoothly and slept better after the massage.

31: EMAIL

JUSTIN WAS SITTING in his favorite spot at the end of the sofa when Lauren got home from work at dusk one day. He had his laptop on the handy little work table that could be put over the sofa, and everything seemed normal. But he was beaming. He looked up at her, his eyes alight. "Guess what happened today!" he said.

"Umm, you can add swimming to your physical therapy?"

"Well, yeah, I can start swimming next week. Guess what else?"

Lauren had no idea. What could make Justin so happy? If Don and Betty were going to have another child, he might be glad for them, but not that much. She was stumped.

"Ace! I got an email from him! He's alive!"

Lauren felt a wave of relief go through her body. "Amazing! Read me the email!"

"Not much to it. I got a kick out of his email address, top of the deck at gmail. He wants to know if law enforcement would be after him if he came back here… He didn't even sign his name or say anything about where he is. I wouldn't be surprised if he's paranoid about what kind of trail he leaves online. Isn't this great? I was going to call you at work as soon as I found out, but I wanted to see your face when I told you."

Lauren moved the piles of papers next to Justin on the sofa, so she could sit there herself. They held hands and smiled into each other's eyes. "I didn't realize till this minute how much his disappearance dragged me down," she said.

"I knew," Justin said. "I've thought of him a dozen times a day. I never stopped thinking that he might have lost his life because of saving mine. The old rivalry hasn't mattered to me since he pulled me out of the creek."

"I think we can find out about law enforcement," Lauren said. "Grace is working at the library this evening. I'll call her now and ask her to check with Paul about how things stand over at the sheriff's department regarding the deaths of Billy and Sylvia."

Grace said Paul hadn't talked about it with her in a while, but she would ask him when she got home from work.

The next morning around breakfast time, Grace called back and said that Ace was in fact the only suspect in Billy's killing but they didn't have much to go by. "If he has an alibi for that night, they will close the case," she said.

"What about the other death, the woman named Sylvia?" Lauren asked.

"Paul said that if Ace had a good alibi for the first one, the sheriff's office would close them both. He said they figured the same person likely did both."

"Thanks, Grace. We'll see what we can find out. See you at work," Lauren said.

She told Justin what Grace had said and added, "I have never stopped wondering if maybe Ace did kill Billy and even the woman too. I remember that I told you what he said to me one night in the library, that he hadn't done it but that if he had, he would have lied to me and said he didn't."

"Sounds like an Ace mind-game," Justin said. "You know I didn't pay a lot of attention to the details while I was in Fort Collins. We'll have to see what we can find out. If I didn't have this doggone leg problem, I'd drive out to the homeless camp today while you're at work and talk to some of the people there. I wonder if Don could take me out there."

Lauren noted to herself that it was the first time Justin had seemed to care about who committed the killings, but she knew it wouldn't be tactful to say that. She said, "He could, I'm sure, but are you supposed to be hiking around in the woods, even with crutches?"

"No, I suppose not. My leg bothered me again last night so I'm inclined to behave myself. But I bet Don would be willing to go out there and talk with people. He knows a few of them from fixing their cars, and I think they trust him because of it. He's probably easier for them to trust than I would be, with my government job. I'll call him pretty quick."

"Great," Lauren said. "Okay, honey, I'll be home for lunch. It's the egg salad in the fridge, so don't eat it for a snack! Outta here…"

Don went out to the camp that afternoon and stopped by in the evening to give them a report. He stretched out on the new recliner and admired how comfortable it was, teasing them with a little pause before saying anything about the camp. "I did see a couple of people I knew, and some others were hanging around the fire. I didn't say anything about Ace's email at first… I just asked what people were thinking about the deaths. Right away, one guy named Jimbo said it's best to just leave it all alone. That put a total damper on the conversation, so then I said that Justin had heard from Ace, who was wondering if it was cool to come back."

Don went on, "That stirred things up. People were thinking he had drowned in the flood too, and a couple of people said they would be glad to see him again. But then Jimbo—he seems to be kind of a leader there—said it could have been Ace who did the killings, and so the sheriff's department might still be on his case. Someone said it could have have been Garrett who did it, and that Garrett was known to have bought heroin before then. But someone else objected that he wouldn't have done it since someone tried that method on him."

Don got out of the recliner. "Overall, I could tell that nobody was going to tell me who had done it if they knew, nobody much cared, and that they were urging caution about what the authorities might do arbitrarily. I asked them if anyone else might have done it, and nobody volunteered any names. One guy said he didn't think Lee could have done it, and some others agreed. Well, I'll be going on home for Rosie's bedtime stories."

"Thanks," Justin said. "That doesn't take us much further, but it's something."

"I admired the ingenious tents out there, some made with several tarps," Don said. "You gotta hand it to those people, how they cope. I promised I'd go out there one day soon and check on some vehicles that aren't running, as a freebie. So if you think of anything more you want me to ask, let me know."

"That's really nice of you," Lauren said.

Don said, "Heck, it's not a lot to do. I don't mind. You never know when you might be the one needing help."

"Amen to that," Justin said.

32: ALIBI

ON SATURDAY AFTERNOON, Momo, Lauren and Betty got together in Momo's living room, around a coffee table laden with a pot of herbal tea and platters of finger food Momo had arranged artistically. They could see into her dining room, now her art studio, and Lauren and Betty admired the two paintings that were in progress. One was a landscape of the rugged mountains outside of Silvermine, realistic enough that you could tell where the place was, yet with a lot of abstract qualities in the way the mountains were depicted. The other was a portrait of Momo's great-granddaughter Rosie, sitting in the dirt, playing with a shovel and bucket, her face happily looking up toward the artist. Bright, pastel colors emanated from Rosie and circled around her.

Betty loved that painting. "It's coming along great, Momo, and it reminds me why I left her home. She's getting to be such a terror in people's houses… she's so full of life that I never know what she'll do next! Don's got her this afternoon. Say, Lauren, how's it going with Justin?"

"He can be grumpy when he gets frustrated by his leg, but I'm grateful that he came through so well," Lauren said. She thought for a moment and decided to share something personal. "I haven't had to worry a bit about his hot old girlfriend in Fort Collins, either."

"You mean he can't…" Betty started to say, but she looked at Lauren's red face and said, "Oh, he can!"

"We can," Lauren agreed. "While he was in the hospital, he applied his formidable intellect to the physics of moving his femur into various positions, I bought a king-sized bed and more pillows, and the results have been great!"

Momo laughed. "I told you not to worry about the old girlfriend," she said. "She's history. Your story reminds me of something that happened last week. Margaret Snow and I were having lunch at that L-shaped cafe downtown, the one with the little bar. We were at one of the tables up front, and we heard some conversation at the bar about one of the men there turning sixty. So when I went past the bar to use the rest room, I asked whose birthday it was. It was a nice-looking guy I didn't know, but he had a good vibe. I just said, 'I remember sixty,' and went on down the hall without saying I was three years older. On my way back, he said that I was in great shape for being over sixty, and after a little more chitchat, he politely asked if I would like to make love that afternoon. I said 'No, but thank you,' I gotta say I was flattered… I think that's the first time I've been hit on in twenty years!"

"You are still a looker, Momo," Betty said. With her reddish hair, curvy but not overweight figure, and clothes that reflected her love of subtle color combinations and good fabrics, Momo was always a pleasure to look at. Even here, just for tea with Betty and Lauren, she was wearing a pale turquoise cotton blouse, nice blue jeans, and a turquoise and blue silk scarf looped over the blouse. Her earrings and shoes were blue. Beyond clothing, there was a vibrancy in Momo's face that said she loved life.

Betty continued, a little shyly, "Well, an old story of mine fits in here. Right when Don and I first got together, one Sunday afternoon I walked from his place over to the grocery store. He and I had been, you know, in bed all morning, and I must have been kind of glowing. In the store, I ran into one of the most popular guys in my high school class—this was a couple of years after we graduated. He had never even glanced at me in school, but he started up a conversation with me and almost right away he asked me to get together with him. He said it in a way that his meaning was unmistakable."

Lauren asked, "What did you say?"

"I can't believe it, but I told him I had just made love with Don Russell and I would be doing it again soon."

"That's hilarious," Lauren said. "I wish I had a good story of someone coming on to me, but I guess being almost thirty is taking me out of that league. I'd have to go back to my college years to think of anything at all."

Momo laughed, "Your age isn't why, dear. You're very attractive and I'm sure men notice you, but you have a vibe of not being available. I can see it in your aura, it acts like a little picket fence. Of course, most people don't see the fence, but any guys looking for a date would sense it without knowing why."

"Except Justin, I hope!" Lauren said.

"Of course. Justin is the reason you have that vibe. How is his leg?"

"It's coming along well, and his spirits are improving. I came home from work the other day and he was really happy. He got an email from Ace that day, and that was the first we knew that he was alive…"

"You should have asked me. I just knew he was, even though we haven't been in touch," Momo said.

"You know, I meant to, but I've been so busy that I didn't get around to it. Taking care of Justin is a big job, even though the rest of the family has been wonderful," Lauren said.

"Where is Ace?" Betty asked.

Lauren said, "We don't know from his email. I don't think he'll come back here any time soon, unless he can come up with proof he didn't kill Billy, like evidence of where he was at the time."

Momo said, "I think Ace was here when Billy died. What day was that?"

"Let's see, it was the first week in October, I think, that Wednesday morning early."

Momo said, "Great, I think I have Ace's alibi. He came over here one afternoon around then and helped me take some of my paintings downtown to the gallery in his van. After that, we went out to dinner and then he stayed overnight in my guest room and did his laundry here. Then as he was leaving around eight the next morning, something happened that could help his alibi. He was going back and forth to his van, which was parked out in the street right in front, taking his laundry and things out."

She continued, "You know the uptight couple who live next door to me? Well, they were going out their front door, on their way to a morning prayer breakfast at about the same time. Ace made a point of greeting them politely, learning what they were doing, and saying how good it was to start the day with prayer…he was putting them on, but the next day, the woman said to me what a nice young man had been at my house. She asked if he was my son, and I said he was like a son to me. I'm sure they would remember that and be able to pin down exactly what date and time their prayer meeting was. Of course, if they were told that he was a suspect in a murder case, they would lock everything up tight and not speak to me again!"

"That's great proof," Lauren said. "Momo, I hope this doesn't offend you, being as how you've been friends with Ace for years, but I've wondered if he might have killed both Billy and Sylvia. And if you have this water-tight alibi, why didn't he say that he wasn't around when Billy died? He must have known he was a suspect."

Momo said, "Ace dances to his own drummer, there is no getting around it. Yes, of course he would have known he was here when Billy died, but he must have preferred to keep quiet about it."

Lauren said, "Aha, I think I have it! Does this make sense? That he thought if it was widely known that he hadn't done the killings, then people would have jumped to the conclusion that Garrett did? When I saw how upset he was when Garrett almost died from the heroin-alcohol combination, I realized how important it was to him to protect Garrett."

"Yes, I agree," Betty said. "That makes perfect sense. But I have to say, he could have left Momo's house in the dark before dawn, driven out to the camp—or even jogged out there, he's a fast runner—done the murder, and been back in Momo's guest room before daylight. That wouldn't have been out of character from how I remember him when we were younger... he was brash and doing things most people wouldn't even think of."

Momo protested, "But I would have heard him. I'm a light sleeper." Lauren noticed that Momo didn't deny that Ace could have done something like that.

Betty said, "I slept in that guest room when I lived with you and I remember the sound of your snoring echoing through the house, Momo."

"Well, you must be right if you remember it that way, dear, but I still think we have a good alibi, whether or not it's exactly what happened," Momo said.

Momo went and got her date book. There, in ink, was an entry about taking paintings to the gallery on a Tuesday afternoon in October. There was another entry in her cash log for the same day that said "dinner with Ace." Lauren remembered the day of the week that she helped Lee send the email to Barb as a Wednesday. It all fit.

"I'll call the sheriff's department and tell them all this," Momo said.

Lauren said, "Justin will be really pleased with this news and he'll email Ace that you've got a great alibi you're going to tell the authorities."

33: READING

"THIS IS A cool idea," Lauren said to Justin one evening as they lounged reading in the living room. He had become a fan of the recliner when he was reading for long periods of time, as it supported both his legs comfortably. Lauren and Mickey were stretched out on the couch, under a new afghan Sue had crocheted recently.

"It's from *The Murder of Roger Ackroyd*, by Agatha Christie. The detective, Hercule Poirot, is talking to a group of people in the house where a murder took place. He says that every one of them is hiding something, whether it's trivial or not. They may be hiding things that supposedly aren't pertinent to solving the mystery… and the implication is that they might be. Well, that got me thinking about Billy's murder."

"Are you still on that?" Justin grumbled.

"Yes, I am," she said. "I think it matters to know the truth. But even if you don't care about that, this is an interesting point about how people act in general."

"That they conceal things from each other? You know that," he said, picking up his Kindle as a not-so-subtle cue that he wanted to return to it.

"Well, sure, I know that we all don't say certain things to each other. You wouldn't discuss your recent bouts of constipation with just anyone."

"No, and I don't appreciate your mentioning it either." Justin was hating that particular side-effect of his pain meds but he wasn't quite ready to go completely off the meds.

"I chose something with an emotional charge on purpose, to try to make the point clearer. Yeah, everyone knows that people conceal things but we mostly think it's just part of life and we don't go around wondering what people are keeping secret."

"I'll give you that," he said. "I truly don't want to know what most people are keeping secret. I'm quite sure that almost all of it is boring and—to pull a word from what you said—trivial."

"Okay, but you are reading thrillers like there is no tomorrow and I am mulling over the deaths out at the camp. If we were each to consider what people are hiding, we might learn something."

"Maybe," he said. "I can see that with the thrillers. But honey, the evidence seems to be that Ace or Garrett or possibly even Lee killed Billy. Now it's likely to be shown by Momo's story that Ace didn't. So that leaves two dead guys. Why keep on with it?"

"I'm just reflecting... bear with me. What about Jimbo, for example? What could he be hiding? It's not just one person, though. What might the woman Vanessa out there know? She seemed very observant. What could you have remembered from when you broke your leg but not thought to mention to anyone? And of course the star player in all this would be Ace. What won't he tell us if he comes back, and how much of what he might say would be literally true anyway?"

"I see where you're going," he said. "Ace does seem to live more in a mythic reality than in the everyday world. As for something I might not have mentioned, actually there is something that came back to me from when I fell in the creek. It is trivial, but I'll tell you. I remember that when I started to slide into the water, I had a split-second choice, whether to go on down with the way the dirt was giving way or to reach out and grab you to break my fall and maybe stay out of the water. I had the instantaneous thought that if I grabbed you, we would likely both end up in the creek, so I didn't."

"Thanks for not dunking me, I guess," she said. "That's interesting and I'm glad to know it. Actually, if you had grabbed me, everything would probably have unfolded differently. Chaos theory, you know."

Lauren thought for a moment. Did she want to push Justin's buttons, as the question in her mind might do? She decided to ask. "That reminds me, I've been wondering how come you've been so caught up in thriller after thriller."

Justin's face showed defensiveness for a moment, and then he said, "At first it was just a way of distracting myself from the pain in my leg, and sometimes I still read for that reason. But I think it's been part of my psychological healing, too. Life feels more fragile now, and it's been absorbing to read these novels where people deal with that edge. "

He continued, "I'm starting to read other stuff, too. I got that book you told me about, the two Christian guys who traveled around for months homeless, and what they learned."

"Yes, *Under the Overpass*. I enjoyed it."

"It had some good parts. I also looked at some books on climate change, but I already knew most of what they said… heck, I could write a better one myself. But it's part of thinking about edges. I suppose that those people who understand that climate change is happening usually have a particular scenario they think about. They recognize the whole planet is getting warmer and ice is melting in many places, all of which is documented, and from that they assume that exact pattern will continue."

Justin shook his head. "But we don't really know that. A book I did read all the way through was called *Apocalyptic Planet*, and it explored a variety of possible futures in a vivid way. The guy seems to be one of those people who only feels alive when he is doing crazy, risky things, and he traveled to deserts and glaciers and wilderness. I've got to give it to him, he tells a good story. Hey, would you pass me the book? It's right under the permaculture one over there."

He opened the book and read out the chapter titles. "*Deserts Consume… Ice Collapses… Seas Rise… Civilizations Fall.. Cold Returns…* and there are several more. The book did remind me that climate change could go various ways, some of them in our lifetimes.

He makes it really clear that the planet is always changing, and that's going to continue whatever people do. It kind of helped me loosen up on my self-righteous stance that humans have to change or else."

Lauren said, "You're learning something new if you think you were self-righteous."

"Wasn't I at times?"

"Yes, sometimes. Say, do you think this book would be a good one to buy for the library?"

"Yeah, I do, but read it first yourself and see what you think."

"Okay," Lauren said. "First I'll finish the cozy mystery I'm reading now."

Justin said. "I won't have as much time for reading next week, because I'll start working for the Forest Service from home."

"Oh, you got that set up? How many hours a week?"

"Just ten or fifteen to start," he said. "With my physical therapy, that seemed like enough to ease back in. It will be good to get back to work on the report I was doing when I had the accident. One of my colleagues has been working on it lately, and we'll collaborate."

"Sounds good," she said, thinking back to Hercule Poirot's point. Justin had concealed things, even if not deliberately. But how easy it was for all of us to live in our own little worlds and not even know it.

34: OMG

"HI, MOM," LAUREN emailed one evening. She rarely saw her parents, even though they lived in Denver, but she stayed in touch with them by email. "I wrote you about how I went out to the homeless camp a couple of times recently. Their situation sure gets my attention, and I've been wondering. Did we ever have homeless friends when I was growing up? Or is there any other reason I'd be so interested?"

She sent the email off but didn't expect an answer soon. Her mother was usually slow to reply to her emails. To her surprise, she got an answer an hour later.

"Well DUH sweetie, of course you'd care. Don't you remember what we did just about every May or June? We moved out of an apartment that we hadn't paid rent on for a month or two, hauled our stuff to a storage place, and car-camped with that big tent we had. Your father is a brilliant man, that's where you get your brains, but he was not so good at holding jobs. Then we camped in the public lands and every fall we got another lousy rental, usually in time for you kids to start school in a new place. You were homeless every summer, baby. We weren't ever totally without food though, thanks to food stamps. Love, Mom"

Lauren sat back in her chair. She read the email again and then again. She sent her mom a reply. It just said "OMG!" She was pretty sure her mother would know that was short for *Oh, My Gosh!*

Of course she remembered all those summers. It had gone on like that until she was in high school, when she got summer jobs and her dad had finally found a more stable position. Maybe her jobs had helped keep her family in a home after that. She'd have to ask her mom sometime.

She had to hand it to her parents, they had made the summers fun. The family was always roughing it, sure. Lauren remembered one time when a black widow spider took up residence in the ladies' outhouse in the campground. She was too scared to go in there and too squeamish to squash it. When she needed to go, she took a long walk to the other ladies' outhouse. She wouldn't even consider using the mens' one nearby, as her mother did. After a while, one of her brothers killed the spider, in exchange for a big stash of candy he knew she had.

But along with memories like the spider, she had so many happy memories, of running around in the woods with her brothers and sister, of sunsets through the trees, of deer coming close, of singing around the campfire and cooking with a Dutch oven in the embers, of long hikes. She guessed those long hikes were likely designed to wear the kids out by bedtime. Well, it had worked.

Just like when they were at home, she always had to help take care of her four brothers and one sister—all younger than she was—but she was allowed to stay up later and read by firelight, flashlight, or an overhead street lamp if there was one. Her parents managed to keep her in library cards, usually with the address of a cousin on them. She would check out stacks of books to take wherever they went. She chose fat books like *War and Peace*, because they were long stories.

Lauren remembered her first boyfriend, a sweet guy from Pennsylvania whose family camped next to hers for a couple of weeks when she was in her early teens. She was allowed to go for walks with him, and they had a favorite place where they would sit on a boulder and kiss. Their last evening together, when they knew his family was leaving in the morning, she let him touch her breasts. She smiled now, remembering her amazement at how exquisite his touch felt. She'd already known the anatomical facts of how babies were made, and she had already decided she didn't want any, but until then, despite all her reading, she hadn't understood why people would bother to make babies.

She got up from her computer and stretched. The email from her mother explained so much. Of course, she felt connected to the homeless. She had known that life too. Her family hadn't camped in the winter, but Colorado mountains got plenty cold during the seasons she had been out there. Lauren remembered shivering from the cold many times, especially early in the mornings when she or one of her parents was starting a fire.

Full of energy, Lauren grabbed Mickey's leash and a jacket, and she took him out for a walk around the neighborhood. She practically danced as different memories came flooding back. Making s'mores. Packing up the tent and helping to tie it on top of the old station wagon when they moved to another camping spot. Washing her hair in cold-water sinks in cement-walled ladies' bathrooms.

When she and Justin had started doing things together, he had been surprised at how much she knew about camping out and how easily she accepted roughing it. She had been surprised that he was surprised, as she took it all for granted.

It was odd, really, that she hadn't thought of her childhood as a reason for her recent fascination with the homeless. She had even mentioned her past a few times, like when she had told Lee that she camped out as a kid. But until she got the email from her mother just now, she had never thought of herself as having been homeless. She thought of how Hercule Poirot had told the group of people that they were all hiding something seemingly inconsequential. Her having been homeless was quite an example, and she'd been hiding it from herself too.

Well, she saw it now, and exuberance filled her. It all made such perfect sense. There was meaning and pattern. She wasn't obsessed, at least not without reason.

When she went back inside, she started talking at top speed to Justin about the email from her mother and how she had been homeless and how it all made sense.

"Whoa, slow down, take it from the top," he said. "You just got an email from your mother, I got that much. How about if you read it to me?"

She did, and bit by bit he got what she was saying.

"But my family camped out a lot too, and you know darn well I don't have any special feelings for the homeless," he said.

Lauren said, as if explaining to a young child, "But, Justin, you were never homeless. Your family always had the house you grew up in, and you could go back there."

"We didn't much, though. We had to bathe in cold streams and stuff like you did, only Silvermine is at a higher elevation than where you were camping around the Front Range, and it was even colder."

"Yeah, I believe you that it was colder, but that's not the point. You're not getting it yet. It was because my family camped out and didn't have any other home, that I felt like I didn't belong anywhere, and that transferred to how I've been feeling about the homeless." Something else occurred to her, "Oh and why I love feeling so connected here in Silvermine! Wow, it's all tied in!"

"I get it, babe. I'm glad you figured it out. Now maybe you can be more rational about things."

"Rational? You do love that word. I wouldn't say this is about being rational, that is left-brain, as much as it is about getting the big picture, left-brain and right-brain connecting."

With that, he did get it.

35: FORWARD

LAUREN COULDN'T WAIT to tell Grace what she had learned from her mother's email. The first chance she had, she blurted out, "My mother just told me that we were homeless at times in my childhood. As soon as I got the email, I realized that every summer when I thought we were just going camping, we were actually homeless. I think that explains a lot."

Grace nodded. "Well, of course it does! What is different for you, now that you know it?"

"I still care as much about homeless issues as I did, but now I can understand why I was maybe a bit obsessed. Now I think I will get it in perspective and get on with other things."

Grace said, "That's wonderful, Lauren."

When the new books on homelessness arrived, Lauren and Grace put them out on the display shelf. Lauren had taken some photos of Lee, who had been flattered and very willing for them to be on the wall in the library. She had turned them into black and white images in Photoshop Elements, the simpler version of Photoshop she used.

She was pleased at how the photos came out, reminding her of some of the Depression-era photos taken by Dorothea Lange and others. She emailed copies off to Barb.

"I wonder if I should print out a Dorothea Lange photo and put it up with these," Lauren said to Grace.

"No, that would only confuse people who didn't know who she was, and I think it would weaken the power of these three photos. You're a good photographer, Lauren."

"Thanks, I've always loved taking pictures. I've been thinking of taking some around the library and submitting them to the newspaper."

Grace said, "How about one of a line of people circling past the bucket that catches the rain right by the circulation desk?"

"Great idea! I'll do that. Do you think it would be cheating to pose some people for the photo?"

"I think it would be better to catch an actual line, with quite a few people in it, because then they could tell their friends it was really like that. It's going to take that kind of word of mouth to get the public keen on a new building. But I bet Ashley could slow down the checkout process some when you're there with your camera."

Lauren chuckled. "She could just chat with everyone more than usual, and I'd have plenty of time to get pictures."

"Speaking of the new building, what do you want to do about that?"

"I think your idea of talking to movers and shakers is a good one. Want to help me make a list?"

"Rotary, Lions, Kiwanis, Toastmasters, groups like that. Churches. Politicians. The school district. Well-known donors," Grace said immediately. She'd been thinking about it.

"Great. I don't think I'd tackle the mayor soon, as he was quoted in the paper as saying that libraries are obsolete. I'll save him for after I've talked with some more sympathetic people. I bet the library board members would have lots of good connections, and I could get some of them to go with me for meetings. Or it might be better to invite the other people to come here, so they'd really see what this building is like."

"Now you're talking," Grace said. "You remember that I'm taking an online course in library outreach? I've got one small project that I'd like to try. How about if I make a list of meeting rooms in Silvermine, complete with any costs to rent them? We can make it a handout, and people will see that there really is a need for more meeting rooms in the town. That will be a plus for the building plan."

"I like it," Lauren said.

36: RETURN

THERE WAS AN old white van parked in front of the house when Lauren got home after the evening shift. She was tired from a full day and looking forward to relaxing with a cozy mystery. But the van had to be Ace's.

Justin and Ace were sitting around in the living room with beers, laughing and reminiscing about high school. A nearly-empty pizza box was on the coffee table. Lauren sat down and picked up a piece. They welcomed her and went right on with their conversation.

"So you were the one who pulled that," Justin was saying. "I should have guessed, but I thought it was the short nerd who always wore plaid shirts."

Ace said, "I wanted to put a confederate flag up the flagpole but that guy beat me to it. But here's one I bet you didn't know I pulled off. Remember when the girls' room on the second floor was fitted out with a set of mirrors that reflected the image out the window and down to the student parking lot? I did that one for our physics classes, but Mr. Wilson refused to give me any credit."

"I did suspect you on that one. I had an idea for how to improve it, though. If you had angled the mirror in the window just a little differently, you could have used two mirrors to send the image both to the parking lot and to the boys' room. I thought of changing it myself but I was too serious to do it." Justin smiled as he remembered.

"Yeah, you were mighty serious. You must have studied a lot for all those tests," Ace said. "That annoyed me, but I wasn't going to lose my cool image by studying. Besides, I was busy learning how to play poker."

Justin said, "It's too bad that we didn't realize then what friends we could have been."

Ace agreed. "No, we had to play it as competition."

Justin reflected, "Well, since you saved my life, I can't be bothered with that old rivalry. I'm hugely grateful to you, man."

"Glad to help out. I would have stayed and made sure you got to the hospital okay, but I was frantic about Garrett. When I could tell that my telepathic message was received by Betty, I just went on up the hill," Ace said.

Lauren said, "What? You sent a message to Betty? I just couldn't imagine how you could leave Justin there by the creek when he needed medical care so desperately."

Startled, Ace asked, "Didn't Betty tell you that I sent her a message?"

Lauren said, "I don't think she knows you sent it. She told Don that she had a bad feeling about a creek running fast, so he and Justin's parents went out to check. They had already told us they'd go out later if we didn't get to dinner."

Ace said, "First I tried to connect with Momo, but I think she was in bed with her boyfriend Arnold right then, because I couldn't raise her telepathically at all, and usually I can. But she shuts off her receptors when she wants privacy."

"This is over my head," Lauren said.

"Shouldn't be," Ace said. "You can do it. In fact, you do it a lot with your dog there. I've picked it up a couple of times since you got here this evening."

Lauren looked at Mickey, who gazed earnestly back at her. They did have a special bond, she knew that much. She'd think about it. "So you must be off the hook with the sheriff's department, if you came back," she said.

"Yeah, they closed the case after Momo talked to them. They didn't even talk to her neighbors. I was going to stay with her tonight, but I don't interrupt when Arnold is there, and I saw his truck this evening when I came down the street."

Justin said, "I told Ace he can sleep on the sofa for a few nights."

Lauren nodded and asked, "Ace, can you tell us more about how everything happened?"

Ace said, "Sure. Billy's lung cancer was getting a lot worse..."

"BIlly had lung cancer?" Lauren asked. "I had no idea. Was that a secret? Justin, that's an example of what we were talking about, what Hercule Poirot said."

"What was that?" Ace asked, and Lauren explained.

Ace said, "It wasn't really a secret, but Barb may not have known it was so far along. He didn't have symptoms except a cough, but then suddenly he was in real bad shape. He wouldn't go to the hospital for fear they would keep him there, but there is a doctor who sees some of the guys from the camp for office visits. He went to him. The doctor gave him some pain meds, and told him what he could expect, more or less. So after that, Lee tried to get Billy to go up to Barb's in Wyoming, but he didn't want to bother her. He told Lee he wasn't going to go crawling home at the end of his life."

Ace took another pull on his beer. "When Billy started having bad pain, Lee asked my advice. I said you could have gotten euthanasia in Oregon, but it was too late to get Billy out there and get residency. Then Lee asked me if I could perform euthanasia on Billy. That surprised me, but Lee said he just couldn't do it. I told him I didn't want the karma. I've seen some of my past lives where I was a soldier, and I'm still cleaning them up."

Lauren thought this was getting stranger.

Ace went on, in a matter of fact manner. "I knew my brother could do it and wouldn't care. He got really messed up in the military. But I didn't feel like suggesting Garrett to Lee. I just told him that probably someone else around the camp could help him out. He and Garrett were already buddies. But Lee and I did talk a little about methods. I said that just about anyone out there could have thought of alcohol and heroin together… so many people have died that way when they didn't mean to."

"So you thought it was Garrett when it happened?" Lauren asked.

"I suspected it and when Sylvia died the same way, I figured it was even more likely to be him. They had been lovers a while back and he still was fond of her…"

"Wait a minute, that would make him kill her?" Lauren broke in.

"Yes, because he didn't want to see her suffering either. It was the same thing, she had cancer, but it was late-stage breast cancer."

"Weird," Lauren said. "But it's falling into place. Unless you are playing with our minds again, Ace…"

"Who, me?" Ace did his best to make his face innocent, but it wasn't a look that came naturally.

Justin asked, "What was the deal with the Crestone conglomerate rocks?"

Ace said, "That started with a poetic idea of Lee's. He asked me one day if I could drive my van to Crestone and collect some of those rocks to use for a memorial for Billy. I said sure, and he and I and Garrett went over to Crestone. You know that little town? It's full of people who are real different, so I like it there. We had coffee at a place where a lot of scruffy guys were hanging out, so we felt right at home."

Lauren noticed that he said that completely without irony.

He continued, "One of those guys told us where to collect rocks, so we brought back quite a few. I gave some to Momo for her yard, and the rest of them Garrett and I stacked in the woods near the bridge."

Lauren asked, "So when you came into the library and said Garrett had almost died, what was that about?"

"When that happened, I wondered if someone else had taken Billy and Sylvia out, and was going to take him out too, but then I thought that Garrett might have seen how easily they both went and decided he wanted to go too. He's claimed for years that he didn't have a life.

That afternoon, we argued for a long time. I told him I could help him get his own van or whatever he wanted, but he just shook his head and said there wasn't anything he wanted. At least I got him to say that he wouldn't kill himself without talking to me more."

Ace said, "But when I heard about the water rising, I figured he would see that as an opportunity to die and that's when I came over here and asked for your help. Garett would have thought he was doing Lee a favor, too. Garrett's always been kind of different."

Look who's talking, Lauren thought.

Ace sat back, drained. "I took it real hard."

37: AWAY

"ACE, THIS FUTON pulls out to make a bed. Want to give me a hand with it? Justin, how about moving yourself out of the way?" Lauren picked up the clutter from the coffee table as she spoke. As she and Ace made the bed, she pointed out to him a pile of books he might like to look through. On top of the stack was *Gaia's Garden: A Guide to Home-Scale Permaculture*, which Justin was currently reading.

Justin said, "Yeah, that's a really good book. Do take a look at it while you are here. But Ace, how did your boots get stuck in the mud?"

Ace stopped messing with the bedding and flopped down on the futon. "Man, I thought I was going to die right there. I raced up the trail after I left you there, Justin—and you gotta believe me, I knew Betty had gotten my message. I even pulled you further up the slope so there would be room if the creek rose."

Justin said, "Yeah, I remember that. It hurt a lot."

"Better than drowning," Ace said. "I could hear the creek running louder as I went uphill, and the trail was getting wetter. Then the trail was underwater. I didn't want to follow your example, Justin, so I took off away from the creek and climbed around to get to where the guys were camping. I was too late. Their campsite had turned into a pond. I saw Lee's body in the water and he looked dead. I still hoped I'd find Garrett. Man, that big flashlight you made me take was great. I shone it all around the area. Water was pouring in from the cattle pond up above, and there was water everywhere. It wasn't running out downstream much yet.

Ace put his hand over his eyes. "Then I recognized Garrett in the water, wearing his blue jacket, some yards away from me. I couldn't tell if he was still alive or not, so I just went straight towards him, hollering his name. I got about halfway to him, over my waist in the water when my boots got stuck. One of them was stuck under a rock, not just in mud. I couldn't get out, couldn't go forward. That was the worst moment, in terms of basic survival instincts. I wiggled and pulled and finally I got myself out of there without the boots.

"I got back on land and by then I could tell that Garrett was dead. I felt his spirit in a quick flash, connecting with me and he said, 'Outta here!' and he was gone. That was a terrible time. I'd been so sure I could save him."

Justin said. "I'm sorry about your brother."

"Yeah, thanks. The pain was so great, I couldn't stand the thought of being around other people who still had their lives. I went nuts. I was chilled and real wet, and I started walking. I started down the hill, on the old truck track, and I went to my van. That was a long walk.

"My van was parked about a mile from the trailhead where you had parked, nowhere near where people camp. I got out of my wet clothes, dried off, and doctored my feet a little. I had the sense to heat up a can of soup to warm myself, and I got my little propane heater going for a while. Then I got into my sleeping bag, had some vodka, and managed to sleep a little."

"You must have gotten to the trailhead quite a while after I did," Lauren said.

Ace said, "I was still above the road when I saw the flashing lights of the ambulance leaving the area and I figured that was Justin. When I woke in the morning, I decided to skip town. I just didn't want to be around anyone, and it didn't help that I knew the sheriff's office might want to question me about the deaths. I did one thing here in town. I phoned the hospital and asked for Justin. They said your room phone was busy, so I knew you were alive. Psychically I had gotten that you were but I wanted to verify it. I thought of running in to see you, man, but I was still so wigged out from Garrett's death that I just left."

"I understand," Justin said.

Ace said, "Then I drove, with no plan for where I was going. I found myself heading south, and I kept going that way since there are farms in northern New Mexico where I know the people. I stopped at a gas station in one of those tiny towns on the road, and loaded up on bread, peanut butter, candy bars, canned soups, bottled water, vodka… just the essentials. I got a bad cold from being chilled after my immersion in the pond. Mostly I slept for a few days, in the national forest there, going away from the highway on some of those little dirt roads, where nobody would find me. I got wasted, mourned Garrett, and railed at the Universe. I don't know how long I was there."

Once they went to bed, Lauren and Justin talked softly about what Ace had been through. As Lauren started to doze off, Justin turned on his Kindle. "I'm wide awake, thinking about all that," he said. "Gotta read for a while."

Lauren woke in the night, hearing voices. Mickey was curled up at her feet, but Justin wasn't in bed. He and Ace were talking in the living room, but with two doors between her and and them, she could only catch an occasional word. The characteristic cadence of each voice said so much about their characters. Justin's voice was much calmer and he laughed more. Ace's voice had a ragged edge.

She thought again of how Ace had told her, that first night he came to the library, that he hadn't killed Billy, but that if he had, he would have lied to her and said he hadn't. How he loved to twist people's minds around. That comment had become the essence of Ace to her.

So how did he fit with the four deaths? His story about Garrett and Lee drowning had rung true to her when he told it, and she could easily enough verify it with the search and rescue guys or maybe Jimbo. Ace had the alibi about being at Momo's the night Billy died, though it sounded like he was the brains behind the method of death. As for the most recent time, when Garrett almost died of heroin and alcohol, she had seen Ace so distraught when he came to tell her, that she wholeheartedly believed his story from that day.

That left her with one unresolved death. What about Sylvia, the woman who had died in the same way as Billy? Lauren thought there could be an element of kindness in the killer's motives but what had Sylvia herself wanted? And had it been Garrett, or had Ace done that one? Lauren thought she could have a chat with Vanessa. Maybe she could take some more of her old clothing out to the camp near the bridge and offer it to Vanessa and the few other women who camped out there. That would be a good way to chat informally with them. She could do that in the morning, as she didn't work till noon, and she could leave the house with Ace not knowing her plans.

Finally, she slept again, to the murmur of voices from the living room.

38: WOMEN

ACE SLEPT LATE. That made it easy for Lauren to get out of the house in the morning, to go to the camp without him knowing it. She didn't want to tell him that she was going sleuthing to find out if he'd been involved in killing Sylvia. She didn't even tell Justin, also fast asleep, about her intention. She just left a note that she had found more clothing to take out. And she had… she collected a few items of warm clothing she didn't really need, bagged them in a garbage bag, went out through the greenhouse, and stuck them in the car. She left Mickey at home this time.

She wondered, herself, why she felt compelled to investigate further. Did she expect to find out anything new about Ace? Probably not. It was just her obsessive curiosity running amok once again, she scolded herself. But that didn't make her turn back.

It was chilly out at the camp. No sun had reached the camping area yet, and there was a light dusting of frost on the ground. Carrying the big bag of clothing, she went to the campfire and accepted a cup of mediocre but very hot coffee from Jimbo. She chatted a while with him, mentioning that Ace was back in town and had spent the night at their place. This time, Jimbo didn't show any negative emotion at the mention of Ace.

"He and Justin were rivals at Silvermine High, never friends," Lauren commented. "But Justin says that since Ace saved his life by pulling him out of the creek, all that is history."

Jimbo nodded. "Not knowing about Ace and losing the other four has been hard on just about all of us. We're being a little kinder with each other."

"Say, do you know where I could find Vanessa? I've got some women's clothing with me."

"She has a tarp tent down that path, the second place you come to." Jimbo waved his arm in the direction he meant.

Lauren found Vanessa making coffee over a tiny cooking fire. She accepted Vanessa's offer of a cup, and wasn't surprised that it was much more drinkable than Jimbo's. The sun was just coming into the clearing, and she and Vanessa stood where the feeble warmth could reach them.

"What brings you out here?" Vanessa asked.

"Well, I found some more old clothing I don't wear," Lauren said. "Warm stuff. Maybe some of the other women here would like some of them too."

"I'm sure they would," Vanessa said. She called out, "Shirley! Joanne! Want some warm clothes?"

A couple of women appeared from nearby tents. One of them was holding a paperback novel in her hand, her finger keeping her place. Once she saw what was going on, she put the book in her tent. Lauren opened the bag and the three women divided up the sweaters, slacks, and sweatpants, putting aside a few things for others who weren't there right then.

After a bit more small talk, Lauren said, "I'm not sure how to ask this, so I guess I'll just be blunt. Do you think Ace might have been involved in any of the deaths? I'm asking you this confidentially, because Ace is staying at our house and becoming buddies with Justin… I just want to be sure that I can feel completely safe."

Vanessa patted Lauren's shoulder. "I'd say you can. Ace likes to mess with people's minds, for sure. You know, he thinks he's so smart, but he isn't the only one with a brain around here. Even Garrett was smarter than Ace ever saw, but Garrett's social skills were so bad that people didn't notice it. By the way, when Sylvia and Garrett were real close, she told me she thought that Garrett stayed wasted all the time because he was so sensitive. That's a little off the subject, though."

Shirley, the woman who had been reading, said, "I don't think Ace killed anyone. My bet would be that it was Garrett who gave the injections. He was always talking about how great life after death would be. He wasn't into regular religion but he could hardly wait to get there. He probably would have sent more of us on ahead if he hadn't gone in the flood."

"You know, they were real secretive about who did it," Joanne said. "I haven't heard if anyone else in the camp saw either Billy or Sylvia getting the heroin. Did Ace tell you about the night Garrett tried to die the same way as them? By putting a rock at his feet and drinking and shooting up?"

Lauren nodded. She would start crying if she tried to talk.

Joanne said, "A couple of guys in the camp didn't let Garrett die, they gave him a shot of the stuff that keeps you breathing and brings you back from overdosing. I overheard him and Ace talking right after that. Garrett was saying that he had been watching both Billy and Sylvia, and that they needed freedom. That was his exact word, *freedom*. He told Ace he didn't have regular cancer but he had something that was like cancer in his emotions, and it hurt him too much. He couldn't bear it and he was ready for his freedom too. I tell you, he was really pissed at the guys who brought him back and at Ace too. He and Ace got into a big argument."

Lauren wiped her eyes. All three of the women were wiping theirs too. She said, "Thanks a lot. I don't have any worries after what you all told me."

She said to Shirley, "Say, I see you like to read. Do come by the library any time. I'll get you a library card to check out some books." She was glad they had made a policy that people without addresses could check out two books at a time.

"I got this at one of those free boxes the library has around town," Shirley said.

That pleased Lauren, as the boxes had been her idea. "We're going to add a box to the homeless shelter in a month or two. Say, speaking of the shelter, how come you are out here instead of where it's warmer, if you don't mind my asking?"

She immediately wondered if she had overstepped a limit, but the women didn't mind her question at all. It seemed that they appreciated the chance to tell their stories. Joanne, the most talkative one, had three teenage children when her husband left them all with no money. She had a lot of run-ins with social services over the kids, and she preferred to stay away from do-gooders, including the people who ran the shelter. She did say she'd go there in the winter if it turned bitterly cold, but she didn't know if she'd get in. The shelter was often full. Her kids were now grown and out on their own. She was proud of them.

Shirley told a similar story. She was a veteran and had a small pension but it wasn't enough for her and her two kids. Now they were living with her mother in Georgia, and she sent them as much money from the pension as she could. She didn't say anything about the shelter, and Lauren wasn't going to push.

Vanessa said, "I had to go to the shelter last winter for a while when I was sick, and it wasn't bad. I just like it better out here with people I trust. Also, I work sometimes at a motel in town, and I can sleep in a workroom they have."

Shirley said, "Vanessa can do all sorts of things. She used to manage motels."

Vanessa said, "Yeah, I did, but the chain I worked for went bankrupt and I lost my job as a manager. I don't tell the motels around here, or they wouldn't even let me clean their toilets! They'd say I was overqualified." She smiled ruefully.

Joanne said, "Life is just the pits sometimes, no getting around it."

Joanne's comment rang in Lauren's ears all day.

39: BUSINESS

RICHARD PAUSED IN his cleaning one morning when Lauren went in early to work. "Barb sends her greetings and she wants to know how things are going with Justin's leg."

"You stay in touch with her?" Lauren was surprised.

"Well, we've been doing a little business together, so we're in touch, mostly by email."

"Business?" Lauren was curious.

Richard turned deliberately vague, leaving Lauren with the impression there was something he didn't want her to know. That was fine… his life wasn't her business. But it felt more like he was keeping a secret than that it was something personal to him. Hey, maybe she was more intuitive than she realized. Well, she'd try to find out more at home tonight from Ace.

"Justin's coming along really well," she said. "His physical therapist said he's the most diligent patient she's ever had. Combining that with his excellent fitness when the accident happened means he's way ahead of the schedule she expected."

"Good for him," Richard said. "And remember to call me, or tell him to call me, if he needs a ride sometime, or any other help." He scribbled his cellphone number on a piece of scratch paper and handed it to Lauren. Obviously, it was for Justin, since Richard knew perfectly well that Lauren had his number on her cellphone. She wondered if there were plans for a late surprise birthday party for her, since it had been on her birthday that Justin's accident had occurred. Something was up.

Well, if it had anything to do with her, she'd know sooner or later, but she was definitely feeling like a victim of what Hercule Poirot had talked about in that Agatha Christie novel. Something was being kept from her, all right. But what could she do about it? Nothing. She turned to work.

Before noon, Margaret picked Lauren up and they drove across town to a nice restaurant that wasn't too pricey. They were having lunch with a fundraising expert. Because the restaurant was away from the downtown area, it was rarely full, so it was a good spot for conversation. Karen Smith, the fundraiser, was a good-looking woman in her forties who had a professional and friendly manner. She and Margaret had worked together once on a project to raise funds for a sculpture in the park, but Lauren hadn't met her before.

Karen knew a lot about grants, and she offered to do grant writing at a discount from her usual fee. She added that if the library had a group of eager volunteers, she would be glad to put on a series of two or three several-hour workshops to teach them what to do. Lauren was pleased with her generosity.

"How interested is the community in a new library?" Karen asked.

Margaret took the lead on that one. "There are certainly a few hundred people out of the ten thousand or so in Silvermine who understand how badly we need one, and many of them would either make donations or get involved. But by and large, I think that far too many people still think the library is fine as it is. I doubt we are close to being able to pass a mill levy for anything like the million bucks that an entirely new building could easily cost."

"Going from complacent to a million dollars can take time," Karen said. "But it's often do-able. You'll want to do surveys for community input… that's something you can do without cost, probably with volunteers you already have. Plus, there are grants available to help you evaluate what is needed. And I'd love to see what architects would say about remodeling and adding on to your charming old building, compared with going for a totally new one."

Lauren said, "I've already chatted a little with some local architects. There are also architects in Denver who specialize in libraries and have designed quite a few around the state."

"It sounds like there is a lot we can do together," Karen said. "Please give me as much advance notice as you can when you'd like to do something with me, as I keep a pretty full schedule."

As they drove back to the library, Lauren and Margaret were stoked by their meeting. "I'll bet she keeps a full schedule," Lauren said. "She's practically the definition of a mover and shaker."

Margaret said, "Really, Lauren, you are no slouch yourself. I'm glad your energy for a new library is on the rise."

"I told you about my discovery that I was homeless part of my childhood, didn't I? Once I learned that, a lot of things fell into place and I think I have a much better balance now."

"Yes, I think you do, too. Say, I had lunch the other day with Virginia Wagner, and we both felt we could remove that probationary period of yours before six months. We just have to get around to scheduling a special board meeting for personnel matters, and make sure the others are on the same page with us. We'll do that one of these days."

Lauren was thrilled. "Margaret! That's wonderful! It will be a great feeling to not have that hanging over my head."

"Yes, I'll be glad to get past that chapter, too," Margaret said with a smile.

Lauren was thrilled all afternoon. She wanted to tell Grace why she was so happy, but she had never told Grace about the probation in the first place, so she couldn't. But she would tell Justin, and he would understand the milestone.

*****

Ace wasn't there when she got home, but Justin said Ace would be back later. "He threw the ball for Mickey in the back yard, so there's no need for a walk. I did my physical therapy already, and I made us a light snack that we can have now and then go frolic in bed. Betty brought by a stew we can heat up afterwards."

Lauren hadn't had anything like that on her mind, but she was charmed by how Justin had arranged everything. She said, "Umm… well, okay!" She was a little taken aback, but she had been wondering how she'd feel making love with Justin if Ace were in the house, given how sounds carried.

They ate the apple and cheese slices that Justin had ready, and then they went to bed for a while. Afterwards, she heated up the stew and made a salad.

"I didn't hear what happened in Wyoming, but I'm guessing Ace told you in the night," she said as they ate.

"He told me that after he left the place where he'd been camping in New Mexico, he worked a few days at a farm near there and earned some gas money. Then he wanted to see Barb, and he phoned her. She said he could stay in their guest cabin. He drove there, going north on the freeway through the Front Range cities, not coming near here. He said they talked a lot and that they got something worked out. I couldn't pin him down on that, but he did say she would be coming to Silvermine for a visit soon."

"She's got to be up to something," Lauren said. "I don't know what's on her mind, but this morning Richard mentioned doing business with her."

She fished around in her purse and gave Justin Richard's phone number. "He seemed kind of eager to help you, maybe give you a ride someplace. That might be an excuse to talk to you… he did push it a bit."

"I'll call Richard and see if he can take me to physical therapy soon. If so, I'll ask him about any secrets going on." Lauren knew he had a great chance of extracting information. That was part of what made him such a good researcher at the Forest Service. Justin might tease her about being curious, but when he got going on a topic, there was no stopping him.

40: MOTEL

"BARB'S COMING FRIDAY," Richard said to Lauren one morning at work.

"She is? Maybe then I can find out what she's been up to."

Richard's background in covert operations made him maddeningly good at keeping secrets. He kept a straight face as he said, "She's putting on a dinner party Friday night for a group of us, and I reserved a private room at the steakhouse. Can Justin and Ace come with you, around six?"

"Sure. Sounds like a don't miss affair. I trust it's not black tie?"

Richard said, "Your jeans don't even have to be clean."

Friday night, Lauren and Justin went in the minivan, and Ace went with Momo. Lauren was surprised that Momo would be going and very curious who else would be there. It didn't surprise her when Jimbo, Vanessa, Vanessa's two women friends, and other people from the homeless camp came in, but she was startled to see Margaret Snow and her husband. Why were library people here? Grace came in a little later, after closing up the library. What an assortment. Richard was there, but Sunshine wasn't in town. There were about twenty people in the group.

The steakhouse meeting room suited Barb, Lauren thought, noticing the old West theme of the paintings on the walls. The tables were arranged to make a long one, like the family-style Basque restaurants that dot the West. Barb welcomed people as they arrived and invited them to sit down right away.

Barb banged her fork on her water glass. "Welcome, everyone. You may not know that I'm pretty good at handling money. All you've seen me do is spend it for Billy's party. Well, I'm spending more tonight, as the tab is on me. And don't go ordering some little salad… go ahead and eat and drink whatever you want, and take your leftovers home."

She sat down and everyone placed their orders. Then she stood again, her gravelly voice easily carrying to the end of the table. "Some of you know what I've been doing in Silvermine but many of you are in the dark. I'm going to tell you now."

She winked at Lauren and said, "When Billy died, I wanted to do a memorial for him, and I wanted it to be something practical. Several of you here told me about what it had been like for Billy to live around Silvermine. He stayed because of his friends, but the winters were brutal. So… well… I talked a lot with my husband and also with Ace and Richard. With their encouragement, I bought a motel here, a run-down old thing that Vanessa has worked at. It was in foreclosure, and it was so cheap that I could pay cash. The timing was great as I had just sold one of my rentals in Wyoming."

She pointed at Ace and Richard. "These two have been masterminding getting things fixed, starting with the plumbing. Ace said he worked on the place as a memorial to Garrett, too. We got rid of the old mattresses and bought new ones plus some more furniture. These two guys hired people to clean and paint every room in the place as well as deal with the junk outside. I think Jimbo did a good bit of that…"

She pointed to him and he waved his hand and nodded.

"It had twelve guest rooms, along with the manager's little apartment behind the office. Vanessa has already moved into that, as she is going to manage the place. Richard is almost finished at the university to be an accountant, and he will be in charge of finances… he won't live there but he'll come around. Seven of the guest rooms will be rented, and they can be singles or doubles. We haven't worked out how much they will cost, but partial work-trades for doing cleaning or repairs will be possible. But accommodations aren't all."

Barb had a broad smile on her face. "I know many of you folks will keep on camping, and so the last three rooms have been combined into a hang-out place we're calling the family room. It has a combination lock to get in. We kept all three of the bathrooms, so you can get a shower or use indoor plumbing when you want. Ace scrounged up a bunch of individual lockers, like kids use in school, so people can keep things there with their own locks. There are sofas and chairs and a television, and a little kitchenette with a large new refrigerator. The wiring has already been checked, and extra outlets put in, so you can charge your cellphones and stuff."

Someone hollered, "Yee-haw!" Lauren thought it was Jimbo, but she didn't see for sure.

Barb went on, "There's a utility room with two sets of washers and dryers. Now I said twelve guest rooms but I've only told you about ten. They fixed up one of the guest rooms in the back to be a workroom mostly for women, with a sewing machine and fabric and crafts supplies. There's a room like that mainly for the guys, with a tool bench. We aren't going back to the fifties in dividing the genders, so anyone can use either, but Vanessa said the women would like a place to hang by themselves at times."

The waiters were bringing in the drinks as Barb stood back, put her hands on her hips, and said, "Now why do you suppose we did all this?"

A voice from the back called out, "You're moving in!"

Amidst laughter, Barb explained. "This is the memorial to Cousin Billy. He and I inherited a ranch in Wyoming from our dads. Billy never wanted anything to do with ranching, and he signed all the papers over to me about twenty years ago and wouldn't take much money. He said he would just drink it. I sold it, as I live on my hubby's ranch, but always figured a good part of the money was Billy's. So I'm calling the motel 'Billy's Place' and I used his money to get it. I just wish we'd done this in time for him to have spent his last days in it."

Warm applause made Barb turn red. "After we eat, we can go over and see the motel. It's about a mile from here, and there is a special surprise there. So just follow my cream-colored SUV, or come by anytime if you can't make it tonight. You all must know where the motels are on the highway just outside the Silvermine city limits, a couple of blocks after where you turn to go out to the camp. One of the guys is at the motel putting up the new 'Billy's Place' sign right now."

Someone asked, "Any rules?"

Barb said, "A few. No heavy drugs. No sex with a minor. Don't leave junker cars there. You folks can figure out the rest, like how much noise you can stand. See, this isn't like an agency-run place. It's more like your home, and that's how I hope we can keep it going. I think we'll keep the county off our backs by still keeping it as a motel... I've got a lawyer working on that part."

Everyone chatted about the motel as they ate their generous portions of steak and veggies. When dessert was served and coffee heated up, Barb stood up again. "Someone just asked me who will rent the rooms and how much they will cost, and I said I don't know. I do know that rooms were offered to Ace and to Jimbo, and they both refused. Ace said he's planning a road trip, and Jimbo said he prefers the outdoors but he'll be coming by the family room, specially when football's on. Oh, I didn't mention it but we've already got satellite for the TV. Vanessa as manager will decide who gets the rooms normally but while it's getting started, she'll talk it over with some other people, to be sure it's fair. There will be some sort of council to deal with all the problems that naturally come up when you have a bunch of people together."

Barb let the buzz die down before she spoke again.

41: SURPRISE

BARB SAID, "ONE more thing. A lot of you know how helpful Lauren has been at the library. Well, you won't have to smell too much when you go there because of the showers you can all use. But anyway, if it hadn't been for Lauren, I just don't know if we would even have gotten the party organized for Billy…"

Lauren was blushing. She hoped Barb wouldn't expect her to give a talk right now. The whole thing had her so blown away that she was speechless. She had had absolutely no clue about the motel and she was near tears at how many problems it would solve. She had already decided to put one of the little library-run free book boxes in the family room.

Barb turned to her. "Lauren, honey, is it okay if I tell them what you told me you learned from your mom?"

Lauren hadn't planned to tell the world, but she just blurted out, "Okay."

"Well, Lauren was emailing her mom about how she was helping the homeless come to the library and about how she'd gone out to the camp. Her mother wrote her back and told her that their family had been homeless a lot when Lauren was growing up. They didn't use that word, but most summers they had to camp out. Lauren told me that when she learned that, so many things fell into place for her. Let's hear it for Lauren!"

Applause filled the room, and Justin put his arm around her shoulder. Lauren looked around and met smiling eyes wherever she looked. Now she felt that she had to speak herself. She stood up and said, "Barb, thanks, that's very kind, but meeting you has really stretched my ideas of how people can care for each other!"

Lauren waited for it to get quiet, and then she got Justin to stand too. He gave her an inquiring look, but she waved her arm upward, so he stood, holding onto his new cane. She said, "Some of you know Justin. He got a broken leg trying to help Ace save his brother and Lee. I'm very proud to introduce you all to my fiancé!"

More applause. Justin stayed standing beside her. "This is the first I heard that we're getting married," he said. "I've asked her to marry me several times, and she has always said maybe. She's never called me her fiancé before, so I have to assume that this is her way of saying yes!" Lauren nodded her head. He pulled her to him and kissed her on her lips. The table erupted with cheers.

Barb said, "You two had better sit down because Lauren needs to be sitting when she hears the next part. Margaret, would you stand for a moment? Margaret is the head of the library board, and they are the people who hired Lauren and brought her to Silvermine a couple years ago."

Margaret stood, with a big smile on her face.

Barb said, "Lauren was super nice to Billy when he went to use the library. She showed him how to do email and she never said an unkind word to him. He wrote me a couple of times about how nice she was to everybody. Then I saw that for myself when I was here, back when we had Billy's party. So I phoned Margaret the other day and told her I was coming to town and about the motel and all, and I said I wanted to do something for Lauren and the library.

"Margaret told me that the library was way too small and that she and Lauren had just met with a lady who does grant writing and fundraising. So I'd like to pay the lady for a while. Margaret set up a meeting for Monday with her, and I'll stick around and we'll make a deal. We'll see how much she can raise for a new library."

Lauren could hardly believe her ears. She couldn't stay sitting, though. She jumped up, ran over to Barb, and gave her a huge hug, then did the same with Margaret. The place went wild.

As everyone got up and put on their jackets, Margaret held on to Lauren. "Come here a moment," she said, and the two of them went into an alcove. "I was going to tell you at work, but this is the time to pile on more good news… a couple of days ago we had a library board meeting for personnel matters, and your record has been expunged." Lauren grinned widely and they hugged.

Everyone followed Barb's SUV over to the motel, which was set apart from other motels in the area by a cluster of trees. It was a typical old motel in being U-shaped around the parking area. Lauren saw a little fenced area with picnic tables, an empty swimming pool, and some pretty rock work done with Crestone rocks.

Vanessa acted as hostess for the tour. She spoke in the professional demeanor she must have developed over years of managing motels. Lauren loved seeing her as friendly as ever but exuding confidence—and nicely dressed, her outfit including a maroon sweater Lauren had given her. Vanessa walked the group through the guest rooms, the family room, and the workrooms. Then she led them to the office door. Barb was standing in the office, and just as you entered it, there was something on the wall, with a cloth over it. Lauren thought it would be a mirror, but why make a big deal over a mirror? She got the idea when she saw Momo slip into place next to Barb.

"Momo painted this," Barb said, as she pulled the cloth away. There was Billy, but not the down-on-his-luck Billy whom they had known. Momo had worked from a recent snapshot of Billy, but she was a visionary artist after all. This Billy was happy and welcoming. One of his arms was gesturing the viewer to come in to the house, and his smile was radiant. The colors around him in the picture went from dark near the bottom to pastel at the top, and they gave a feeling of what he had gone through in his life. Lauren thought it was the best portrait Momo had done. On the frame, it said, "Welcome to Billy's Place."

Momo said, "I'm also going to do paintings of Lee, Garrett, and

Sylvia, but I need photos. If anybody has some, even a cellphone one, please tell Vanessa or call me."

Lauren was not the only one blinking back tears. On the way home, she asked Justin if he had known about the motel.

"Yes, that's why Richard got in touch with me," he said. "He got me involved in designing the memorial fountain that's out by the play yard. He drove me over there one afternoon when you were working, and he and Ace built the fountain, while I supervised. It was made with Crestone Conglomerate rocks Ace had collected. They got it mortared together and they will run it in the spring. They didn't really need me, but it was a nice way to include me. Also, then I could make sure you didn't make any other dates for tonight."

Lauren asked, "Memorial for...?"

"Garrett," Justin said. "Ace buried his ashes under it. Barb and some others took Lee's ashes out to the forest where they had scattered Billy's, and they scattered Lee's there too."

"It's amazing," Lauren said.

"What?"

"All of it," she said. "Every bit."

42: BYE

WHAT WAS THE aroma? Meat, spices, onions… Lauren noticed the heavenly smells when she opened the front door as she got home from work. Had someone brought over a casserole that the guys had put in the oven? Justin was walking with a cane more now, but he hadn't gotten back into real cooking. The combination of standing and reaching and balancing was still beyond him.

Both guys, Momo, and Mickey were in the kitchen. Justin was sitting at the table, cutting board in front of him, slicing veggies and putting them in the salad bowl. Mickey was on the floor, watching avidly, ready to dash after anything that fell. Momo was watching from the window seat. But it was Ace who drew her attention. Wearing her flowery apron over his paint-splattered jeans and faded plaid shirt, he was vigorously stir-frying the source of those heavenly smells. He'd found her huge wok tucked away on a shelf, and he'd filled it very full. He also had her rice cooker going, with a big batch of brown rice.

"Wow!" she said. "This is fabulous. Ace, I didn't know you could cook like this. Why so much… is anyone else coming over?"

"Nobody but Momo. I just walked over and kidnapped her," Ace said. "I don't cook very often, but when I do, I make enough for a bunch of meals. I'm going to take the leftovers out to the camp tomorrow, on my way out of Silvermine."

"Where are you going?" Lauren asked. "I didn't know you were leaving."

Ace laughed. "You want to make this threesome in your house permanent? Let me join you two in that king bed and I'll consider it."

Lauren said, "Ace, you are incorrigibly obnoxious! Let me set the table. How about wine?"

Soon, they were feasting on Ace's concoction. It had an ethnic quality to it, with the variety of foods cooked together in the wok, but he said he just made it up. "You can call it homeless stir-fry if you want," he said. "I always start with onions and garlic and then I add a whole lot of veggies, cut up pretty small… carrots, broccoli or whatever else there is. For meat, I go for ground lamb, like tonight, or pieces of chicken, or whatever else looks cheap and good at the market. If no meat is cheap, I use beans instead. I make it with any kind of rice and with whatever spices strike my fancy, but always a lot of spices."

"I think I'll add it to my repertoire and name it after you," Lauren said. "Hey, we had the meeting with the fundraiser and Barb today. They hit it off great and Barb is going to fund Karen part-time for up to six months. Not only that, but she said that if Karen found any matching grants, to let her know and she'd see what she could do to help! Barb said to say goodbye to everyone. She left for home after lunch and said she'll be back soon."

"That's fabulous news!" Justin said. "Ace has news too, but he wouldn't tell Momo or me anything about his plans till you were here."

"Okay, it's not that big of a deal, I just didn't want to go through it more than once," Ace said. "Like I said, I'm taking off. There's nothing here for me. Everywhere I look, I just remember when Garrett was there too."

Momo said, "Let your pain open your heart, Ace. Not all at once, it doesn't work that way, but bit by bit."

"You sound like Ram Dass," he said.

"Yes, I've learned that he's right about a lot," Momo said. "Funny thing, I just picked my battered old copy of *Be Here Now* to give you." She handed it to Ace, who glanced through it for a moment.

Then he pulled out something he had stuck under a cushion at the window seat.

"While we're giving books, here's one about permaculture for you," he said to Justin, handing him a copy of *Growing Food in the Southwest Mountains*. "One thing that's cool about this book is that every copy is printed at the author's house. She has help, but still…"

Lauren grabbed the book and flipped through its many pages. "Lots of work," she said. "But it does fit the do-it-yourself ethos. Maybe I'll get a copy for the library."

"That looks really good," Justin said, deftly pulling it back out of Lauren's hands and skimming the table of contents. "Maybe you'll come back to Silvermine sometime and see if we've done anything with permaculture."

"After we talked about permaculture in the middle of that night, I happened to see this book," Ace said. "Hey, maybe you could grow industrial hemp. There's a real need for it."

"I'll look into it," Justin said. "I don't think it would have crossed my mind."

"What are you going to do, Ace?" Lauren asked. "Barb announced you had a road trip in mind."

"Yeah, I'm going to Nevada. I'll hit some casinos and play poker. With poker, the higher the stakes, the more knowledgeable your opponents are, because there are plenty of guys seriously trying to make a good living that way. Some women too. I'm not about getting rich quick so what I do is play in the lower levels, where most of the people are ignorant about the nuances of the game. It takes me a while to get a nest egg, but I'm charming as I can be, and people don't mind losing to me. I can tell with my intuition when to quit."

Lauren wondered what Ace would be like in non-stop charming mode. She found it impossible to imagine.

"After high school I was in a group for a while that played blackjack, but I got tired of working with other people and also of being kicked out of casinos. Made some pretty good money, but I got to prefer playing poker on my own," Ace said.

"So you're a gambler?" Lauren asked, with an edge in her voice.

"No, not at all. This is a business for me, no emotions, no crazed eagerness to win, no addiction. I walk away whenever I want to. If you want to call me names, people sometimes call me a card shark. Hey, that's better than what Billy called me, a bad man."

"Better how?" she asked.

"Well, a card shark implies skill. Billy was just mad because I was messing with his mind, but anyone could have done that. He didn't have much mind left by then."

Momo was clearing the table and Lauren figured Justin had already had plenty of time to talk with Ace. She would continue her questioning.

"You told me one time that you don't need much money," Lauren said.

"Don't believe everything people tell you," Ace said. "I've told you that before."

They all laughed and woke Mickey up. He barked and went back to sleep under the table.

Ace continued, "I remember telling you that I need little money, and it's usually true. I'm going to Nevada for two reasons. One, when I'm playing poker, I totally concentrate and so I'll get Garrett out of my head. Two, I'm going to upgrade to an old RV-style van or maybe an eighties Toyota Dolphin, some sort of little rig that has a kitchen and a bathroom with a shower as well as a bed area that isn't the table. A big part of why I hung around the homeless scene was to keep an eye on Garrett. Now that I don't have that reason, a few more creature comforts in a vehicle are fine by me."

As they sipped the tea that Momo had just made, Lauren said, "You once told me that I could probably understand how society is really set up if I hadn't been brainwashed. I thought maybe you were going to go into secret international cabals but actually we never got to that subject. I'm curious what you were going to say."

"You really want to know? I'll give you the short version. I think most people, rich or poor, are clueless about life. Greed for power and money dominates the rich, including your cabals which do indeed run things. But I gotta soften all that with the fact that there are warm-hearted people in every class and place. But I see the poor being shafted throughout history and it's nowhere near stopping now."

He carried on, "I am certain the global climate is getting more erratic. Human activities have sped up the climate change, and I think it's going to get hotter though it still could flip to another ice age. Between the housing crisis which creates so much homelessness, the government creating money out of thin air, and a few other stupidities, the economy is trashed. With the climate changing, a lot of places will be trashed more, including Colorado. Here, drought and forest fire is what I expect mainly, despite this fall's flooding."

Ace took a deep breath. "I've thought all that for a while, and in the past couple of years I've read about Buddhism and I really go for the idea that all of this reality is illusion. But I don't do their practices —not with a mind always in overdrive like mine is."

Justin said, "I agree with some of what you've just said, and you know I care about climate change, but I'm more into making a difference with my life than you are."

"I haven't bought into the illusion that you can make a difference," Ace said, smiling and looking sideways at Justin.

Lauren couldn't resist saying, "So you prefer to buy into the illusion that you can't make a difference."

"Good catch," Ace said to her. "Yeah, the need to be independent does run my actions. But look, I tried to save Garrett and I couldn't."

Lauren felt his sadness but she wasn't going to miss what could be her last opportunity to ask Ace the key question. "So who killed Billy and Sylvia?"

"You must have figured that out," Ace said.

"Maybe, but you could have snuck out of Momo's house and back in…"

"I didn't think of that possible scenario," he said. "Look, I'm not a killer. I'm a trickster. I get off on messing with people's minds. I don't care about being called a bad man because it's a game to me. Garrett was more of a fighter than I was, even when we were kids. The army turned him into a killer."

"So he killed Billy and Sylvia?" Momo asked.

Ace looked at her. "Of course, Momo, one split-second of your psychic awareness should have shown you that."

"I prefer not to open my mind to some things," she retorted. "I was pretty sure of it, though."

"I wasn't sure who did the killings," Lauren said.

Ace stared hard at her for a moment. "Well, not that you deserve it, but here's the closest I can come to proof. Sylvia's best friend at the camp sent me a few photos she had taken on her cellphone, because she knew I'd want the ones of Garrett and Sylvia smiling when they were lovers. But take a look at the last one."

He found a photo on his cellphone and passed it to Lauren. She gasped. It showed Sylvia holding her arm up in the air and smiling at Garrett while he gave her an injection. There was one of the Crestone rocks at her feet.

Lauren figured the photo could theoretically have been photoshopped, but she thought that it was real. It showed Sylvia as a definite part of the action. Finally, Lauren could let go of the suspicions she had had about Ace ever since she met him. What a relief. He was a card shark and a trickster, and Billy probably wasn't the only person to have called him a bad man. But Ace wasn't a murderer.

"I didn't realize it, but till I saw that, I was holding back on being your friend," she said.

"I knew you were holding back," Ace said. "If we're friends, I guess I can't mess with your mind so much. That's too bad, but I probably need friends more than I need victims. I'll find plenty of those in

Vegas."

Justin said, "Ace, I've told you this before: since you saved my life, I've only thought of you as a friend. You are welcome back here anytime."

Lauren nodded. "I've never had a bad man as a friend. It could be interesting."

Ace said, "So if I had killed Billy and Sylvia to end their sufferings, as Garrett did, I'd be a murderer and you wouldn't be my friend?"

"Don't believe everything people tell you," Lauren said. "I learned that from a friend today." They all laughed again. Mickey woke up for a moment and gave a short bark.

She couldn't help asking, "But did Billy know, like Sylvia did?"

Ace shrugged. "Wondered if anyone would ask. The answer is no. Garrett told me afterwards that he couldn't bear to watch Billy, and he said that Lee was crying all the time, so he decided on his own to take Billy out. You probably remember that Lee had asked me to do it and I'd said no. I don't think he asked Garrett, because Garrett probably would have told me if he had, and he didn't.

"Sylvia obviously was involved in her own death. She asked Garrett if he could do it for her, not even knowing for sure if he had killed Billy, and she gave him the money to buy the heroin. She was close to the end and in a lot of pain."

Justin said, "This is all pretty intense, no doubt about it. Ace, have a good road trip and let us hear from you now and then, by phone or that mysterious email of yours."

Ace said, "I can't promise a thing, but you guys and Barb are the only people in this world I count as my true friends, so whaddya think?"

Lauren thought his eyes were glistening.

Momo said, "Remember the painting I did of you, Ace? I bet that some day the colors around you will lighten up. When they do, come back and I'll paint you again."

43: DREAMS

WITH ACE GONE, life at home was quieter. Lauren came home one evening to find Justin wearing nice beige slacks, a light blue shirt, and a dark brown sweater vest. He looked great, but why was he out of his casual jeans? It couldn't be anything bad because he was smiling.

"We have a dinner reservation in fifteen minutes, at the new French restaurant," he said.

She said, "Mickey needs his walk first…"

"Already did that," Justin said."Well, I threw the ball for him in the back yard till he wouldn't play. Now get yourself into something cute and let's go."

The French restaurant was charming. Smelling the cooking aromas as they walked in the front door was a great start, and they were given a good table in a secluded corner. Lauren liked the white damask tablecloths, chilled silverware, the filigree basket of French bread on the table, the long wine list, and *La Vie en Rose* playing softly in the background. Justin dug right into the bread. Lauren's wheat sensitivity wasn't as bad for white flour as for whole wheat—she guessed it was because it had less life force left—and she nibbled on a piece too.

As they sipped their wine, Lauren said, "Did I ever tell you about the conversation I had with Momo about us when you were still in Fort Collins? She sees our auras intertwined. Yours was more green and mine more golden and they were twirled around like the dough in a cookie."

"She sure has different ideas," Justin said. "Never thought of you as my cookie dough. Did she say what we tasted like? Hmm, what part of you should I taste first?" Playfully he reached out for her arm.

"Hey!" she said.

"Okay, you want me to be good, I'll be good... for a while," he said, lowering his eyes to gaze at her chest. She had changed into a low-cut, close-fitting long-sleeved knit shirt, with a paisley pattern. She felt goose bumps from his look.

Justin turned serious. "This dinner isn't only to seduce you at a fancy place. I have some dreams I want to talk over with you. As you know very well, I've had far too much time to lie around thinking since I broke my leg, specially when I can't sleep at night. Hard to believe how recently it happened... it seems like time has both slowed down and sped up. Anyhow, my thinking about my life has been changing. Honey, I haven't had a chance to tell you, but the idea of working full time at a desk in the Front Range isn't so appealing to me now. I've been appreciating Silvermine and living near my family. The way you all rallied around to help me out was incredible."

Lauren stared at him. Justin continued, "So I am thinking more locally. I haven't talked with my folks about this yet, but a few years ago they offered Don and me parts of their forty acres. I talked with Don and Betty the other day, and Don said he wants to stay in town, close to his auto shop. Betty said she would like to help with gardening out at the ranch, but she wants to raise Rosie in town and she doesn't want to leave her own garden."

His eyes were alight as he continued, "I've been thinking about taking over the back twenty acres—it's already deeded separately at the county—and growing food for local consumption. You know the book on permaculture I've been reading, *Gaia's Garden*? Reading it is giving me lots of ideas of how we could use the land to create a little eco-system where food crops would be part of it. But then reading more made me realize I couldn't do what I would want to just on the weekends if I were commuting from Fort Collins."

"Where did you get that book?" Lauren asked. She knew the library didn't have it.

"Betty brought me her copy when she came by one time. After I read a little, I knew I wanted my own, so she got me one at the bookstore downtown," Justin said. "Ace read through it and thought it was cool."

"You'd be happy as a full-time farmer?" Lauren asked.

"Probably not, but here's another part. I've been emailing with my boss in Fort Collins, and we've been exploring how I could either remain a Forest Service employee part time or perhaps contract to do the same kind of writing I do now but from here. It would be a pay cut but still workable, I think. Someone there would do the library research and interviews, then collaborate with me. I'd have to go there sometimes."

"I love it!" Lauren said. "Sounds like we both would get to have our cake and eat it too! So we'd be in Silvermine mostly… I'd work at the library and you would be writing for the Forest Service and doing permaculture, whatever that is."

"It's a way of using the land where you…" Justin began. "No, hang on, that's a whole other conversation, or a lot of conversations. Back to you and me. My boss in Fort Collins came up with a possible schedule. Once I can get around by myself—I'm hoping January—I'm going back to work there for a while. I'd probably hire some help with housework and errands, so I'd work full time and still have time for a lot of swimming and physical therapy."

Lauren frowned.

Justin said, "I wouldn't be there too long, maybe a few months. I might even work full-time for longer and build up a nest egg, provided I can live here part of the time. They are being more accommodating, since I broke my leg!"

"I'd say so," Lauren said. "They weren't open to any of that before. It's okay with me, as long as you stay away from that hottie."

Justin said, "She'll run away when I tell her we are getting married. Hey, when do you want to do that?"

"After you're back here for good, for sure," Lauren said. "I'd like a simple, homemade wedding, in the back yard or maybe out at the ranch."

"We'd have to wait a while before the permaculture would start looking good, and we haven't even talked about whether to stay at your house or move out there."

"My house, I mean our house, of course," Lauren said. "Maybe out there sometime later, but I'm not in any hurry to give up being able to walk to work."

"Yeah," Justin said. "That's fine with me too. I want to talk the permaculture idea over soon with my parents and Betty and Don. I'm going to start sketching out some ideas, and I'd like to get started doing a few things in the spring."

"I want to read that book," Lauren said. "But honey, even before I get to it, we're on the same page at last."

~~~ The End ~~~

"After you're back here for good, for sure," Lauren said. "I'd like a simple, homemade wedding, in the back yard or maybe out at the ranch."

"We'd have to wait a while before the permaculture would start looking good, and we haven't even talked about whether to stay at your house or move out there."

"My house, I mean our house, of course," Lauren said. "Maybe out there sometime later, but I'm not in any hurry to give up being able to walk to work."

"Yeah," Justin said. "That's fine with me too. I want to talk the permaculture idea over soon with my parents and Betty and Don. I'm going to start sketching out some ideas, and I'd like to get started doing a few things in the spring."

"I want to read that book," Lauren said. "But honey, even before I get to it, we're on the same page at last."

~~~ The End ~~~

"Betty brought me her copy when she came by one time. After I read a little, I knew I wanted my own, so she got me one at the bookstore downtown," Justin said. "Ace read through it and thought it was cool."

"You'd be happy as a full-time farmer?" Lauren asked.

"Probably not, but here's another part. I've been emailing with my boss in Fort Collins, and we've been exploring how I could either remain a Forest Service employee part time or perhaps contract to do the same kind of writing I do now but from here. It would be a pay cut but still workable, I think. Someone there would do the library research and interviews, then collaborate with me. I'd have to go there sometimes."

"I love it!" Lauren said. "Sounds like we both would get to have our cake and eat it too! So we'd be in Silvermine mostly… I'd work at the library and you would be writing for the Forest Service and doing permaculture, whatever that is."

"It's a way of using the land where you…" Justin began. "No, hang on, that's a whole other conversation, or a lot of conversations. Back to you and me. My boss in Fort Collins came up with a possible schedule. Once I can get around by myself—I'm hoping January—I'm going back to work there for a while. I'd probably hire some help with housework and errands, so I'd work full time and still have time for a lot of swimming and physical therapy."

Lauren frowned.

Justin said, "I wouldn't be there too long, maybe a few months. I might even work full-time for longer and build up a nest egg, provided I can live here part of the time. They are being more accommodating, since I broke my leg!"

"I'd say so," Lauren said. "They weren't open to any of that before. It's okay with me, as long as you stay away from that hottie."

Justin said, "She'll run away when I tell her we are getting married. Hey, when do you want to do that?"

FROM THE AUTHOR

DEAR READER,

I hope you've enjoyed reading *Bad Weather, Bad Man* as much as I've enjoyed writing it. (Well, actually I hope you enjoyed it more... I find writing to be roughly equal parts of delight and difficulty.)

This is my second cozy mystery, and I'm already working on the third one (which features Lauren's dog Mickey) and making notes for the fourth and fifth ones. It's an interesting challenge to write a series. In this book, I allude to events that happened in the first book, *Dead in the Stacks*.

Homeless people typically use more colorful language than you will find here. Cozy mysteries, such as this one, generally avoid strong language, so I left it out.

Since cozies are generally feel-good books, when my fingers typed the first paragraphs and I discovered that I was going to be writing about homeless people, I wondered how that was going to work out. As the character of Ace developed, I had fun with his view of the world. Like Lauren and Justin, I agree with a few but not all of his attitudes. (Actually, he reminds me a bit of my father, not at all in the specifics of his attitudes, but in a fondness for saying provoking things.)

Also, as a librarian and a library board member, I've dealt with these issues in libraries, as most librarians have by now. One time, I was a children's librarian in a small city library and working the morning of Christmas Eve. A patron we'd had trouble with before came into the children's section waving around a nearly-full bottle of apricot brandy with its cap off. A few drops fell on picture books for preschoolers before I managed to coax him to leave the building or I would call the police. I could tell other stories but that's my most aromatic one.

Please visit my website zanahart.com where you can sign up for my occasional emails, read about what's coming next, see recipes and crafts instructions in more detail, contact me, and so on. There are links to the books and websites I used in doing my research, too.

—Zana